Your Kid Ought To Be In Pictures

"The key to success is the dedication to which one employs energy towards the goal. The road to success can only be measured by how far one has ably walked its path."

— Kelly Ford Kidwell and Ruth Devorin

Your Kid Ought To Be In Pictures

A How-To Guide for Would-Be Child Actors and Their Parents

By Kelly Ford Kidwell and Ruth Devorin

lone eagle
PUBLISHING COMPANY
Los Angeles, CA

YOUR KID OUGHT TO BE IN PICTURES   A How-To Guide for Would-Be Actors and Their Parents
© 1997 by Kelly Ford Kidwell and Ruth Devorin. All rights reserved.

LONE EAGLE PUBLISHING CO., LLC™
2337 Roscomare Road, Suite Nine
Los Angeles, CA 90077-1851
Phone: 800-FILMBKS • Toll Free Fax: 888-FILMBKS
www.loneeagle.com & www.eaglei.com
Printed in the United States of America
Cover design by Lindsay Albert

Library of Congress Cataloging-in-Publication Data
Kidwell, Kelly Ford,
        Your kid ought to be in pictures : a how-to guide for would-be child actors and their parents /
by Kelly Ford Kidwell and Ruth Devorin.
                p.   cm.
        Includes index.
        ISBN 0-943728-90-8 (pbk.)
        1. Performing arts—Vocational guidance—United States.   2. Child actors—United States.
I. Devorin, Ruth - . II. Title.
PN1580.K54   1997
791'.023'73—dc21   97-10416
                                        CIP

iv

Contents

Preface

California and New York are mentioned often throughout this book because they are the most active states for the movie industry. Of all the states, however, California remains the movie capital of the world. The Screen Actors Guild represents over 84,000 professional actors and performing artists working in the entertainment industry today. Approximately 46,000 of these performers live in the greater Los Angeles area. New York is the second largest membership area with almost 25,000 members. Florida is third with 4,000 members, followed by Chicago with 3,000 and San Francisco with 2,500. SAG also maintains branches in Atlanta, Boston, the Carolinas, Dallas, Denver, Detroit, Honolulu, Houston, Las Vegas, Nashville, New Mexico, Philadelphia, Phoenix, San Diego, Utah and Washington D.C. Members in other geographical areas are served through the national SAG office as well as local AFTRA (American Federation of Television and Radio Artists) offices.

The material set forth on these pages can be translated into the language of any state in the country where the entertainment industry is found.

The movie industry is growing rapidly from coast to coast and from border to border. The guidelines concerning breaking into the industry will vary only as they pertain to the requirements under the law of each state in connection with work permits, social security numbers and the like. The mechanics of how to break into the business and the names of the regulating government agencies will remain the same no matter where you live in the United States. If you have any questions, please contact the SAG office in your area.

Acknowledgments

We would like to thank the countless moms, dads and young actors (past, present and future) whose need for the information in this book inspired us to write it.

A very special thanks to our families and friends for their patience with us while we were writing this book and to the Screen Actors Guild for its generosity and wisdom.

Last but not least, thanks to our actors, Krystin Alexis, Ping Apaiwongse, Carlee Ann Bates, Lycia Carruthers, Nathan Carruthers, Jeffrey Caton, Michael Robert Chacon, Katrina Contreras, Christopher Ford, Chuck Ford, Del Ford, Drew Ford, Mike Ford, Mimi Rae Ford, David Guglielmi, Raushan Hammond, Leann Heng, Savannah Houser, Hillary Kidwell, John Kidwell, Melissa Kidwell, Melissa Ann Martin, Stephanie Mason, Kelly McLean, M.D. McLean, Tyler McLean, Eric Terrell Medley, Austin Myers, Julia Myers, Justin Myers, Kara Myers, Andrew Newman, Jessica Newman, Kim Newman, Rebecca Ruth Newman, Lain J. Patania, Katie Persons, Chandler Rendl, David Shahar, and Parker Wilhelm for the contribution of their photographs.

God bless them everyone!

Authors' Note

There is a lot about the entertainment industry that you can only learn from first-hand experience. The best way to gain first-hand experience is to be open-minded enough to let it sink in once you've been exposed to it.

Yes, there's room in the industry for young actors to make a mistake or two, after all, we are talking about <u>children</u>, but a mistake should be something your child learns from; not the inauguration of a bad habit that ends up echoing throughout your child's career.

Of more importance is whether or not you and your child are having fun. If you aren't, you shouldn't be doing it. There is so much jubilation to be had in the industry if you go about it correctly. Like skydiving or accounting, show business is not for everyone. As you may soon realize, it takes tremendous allegiance, a passion for performing and the persistence of Job to catapult oneself to a modest career, let alone one of fame and fortune. If it was effortless—as some people make it look—then everyone would be doing it.

When we say something could <u>never</u> happen, sometimes it <u>does</u>. But we don't want you to be misled about the "norm." There are standard procedures in this industry. To give you a list of the exceptions to the rules would be a total waste of your time and ours because there is no way to define when and where an exception will take place. The best way for you to succeed in this industry is to be aware of how things are most <u>often</u> done.

We wish all of the young actors of tomorrow a gratifying and triumphant ride to their endeavors. May all of you book your first calls and may all of your TV pilots go to series. As for the parents of these young hopefuls, we wish you the very best of luck . . . 'cause you're going to need it!

See you in the waiting room!

Read This First

Before you begin, we would suggest you read this text with a pen in hand, as you will want to highlight important information along the way. We have inserted a blank page after each chapter for your notes and comments.

Rather than raising the issue of gender with he/she his/her references, we will refer to all actors as "he" and all agents as "she." One's gender has pertinence on neither the information, nor the outcome produced by the use of that information.

1

Assessing The Situation

Let's be realistic. If you're honest with yourself, you'll admit that it's <u>your</u> idea to get your child in show business. Whether it's a career as a nuclear physicist or a career on the silver screen, it's a safe assumption that, for most of you, such a proposal first springs forth from <u>you</u>, the parent. Child actors are shaped by their parents as readily as the kid whose parents tell everyone their son is going to be a doctor. There's little chance that this child will be anything less than a full-fledged, tonsil-prodding, doctor. The only difference between the would-be doctor's parents and the would-be actor's parents is that the doctor's parents expect him to be a doctor when he's a grown-up. The actor's parents expect him to be an actor now. Today.

It's tough enough in this day and age for a child to grow up as a regular kid, let alone one in the business. But it can be done successfully. Your only requirement . . . your child must want to do it. And, not to please you, but to please himself.

It's a plain and simple fact that the majority of children from birth to eighteen years don't beg their parents to be put to work. If they did, they'd more likely want to be firemen or secret agents —

anything that, in their young minds, affords a high level of adventure, requires tremendous courage and includes little of what they label as "work." We all know children who plan on being Batman when they grow up.

Don't be enticed by how effortless acting may look on the screen. We'd be negligent if we didn't tell you that, from the get-go, having an actor in the family is nothing less than a mountain of hard work! Not just for you and your child, but for your family, friends, relatives, teachers, agents, producers, directors, casting people and countless others. No child actor wakes up one morning and decides to launch a career in the industry by himself.

We have elected to focus on the child actor whose age range is from birth to fifteen years. A child who is of driving age usually can manage his own schedule and needs less of his parent's time to facilitate his career. Keep in mind, however, that every child under eighteen is a minor and requires adult supervision on the set and a guardian to sign contracts. The information contained herein will be helpful to your teenage wanna-be actor as well as for you parents with younger children. The process for breaking into the industry, as well as matters concerning industry laws, unions, regulations and work permits, remain the same for all children under eighteen who have not been declared emancipated through the courts.

No matter how old your child is, having a young actor in the family will sooner or later envelope the energy of nearly everyone who knows him, especially after he starts working. While it's true that there are a few who are born with a deep-rooted longing for the business, the success of the child actor today is usually due to the efforts of someone else's ambition (most often, his parents). While most child actors today are not "born in a trunk" (a term you rarely hear today), they are capable of handling very successful and prosperous careers.

In the early days of vaudeville (before television or movies), successful adult performers spent most of their time performing on the road with live stage shows. There was seldom a thought of "maternity leave". . . the show must go on. These old-time performers often were forced to use their travel trunks and suitcases as makeshift cribs for their new arrivals. In turn, the children of these performers spent the early part of their lives nestled on top of a costume or two, breathing the sweet smell of greasepaint and face powder. As soon as these "born in a trunk" kids were old enough to execute a proper buck-and-wing, they joined the family act. There was no issue to reflect or values to weigh; these children were, what was then called, natural-born performers and they took to the stage effortlessly. While young actors such as these used to exist in droves, they are few and far between today.

The child actors of today are most often spawned from well-meaning people who stop an unsuspecting parent one too many times in the supermarket to say, "What a cute baby! You ought to put him in commercials!" or, "My goodness, your baby is cuter than the Gerber Baby! He should be in the movies!" The movies? Wow! What a magnificent idea! The parent's response is usually something like "I know. Everyone tells me that. People have been saying it since he was born." What the parent's response should have been was, "Yeah, well, thanks for the tip, but it's easier said than done!" It's not because the task is so difficult, but because the dedication you must have to succeed in the entertainment industry is tremendous and something that would-be stage parents rarely contemplate beforehand. The one condition that remains constant among all show business children—past and present, born in a trunk or not—is that not one of these children ever got anywhere on under his own steam. Not even in vaudeville! Every one of them had parents and agents and families and friends who motivating, training and molding their talents and careers.

Okay, so you've heard all of this a million times! You know it's hard work but your interest is piqued. Well, if that's how you feel about it, it's too late to turn back now! You're riding on a runaway stagecoach and you've dropped the reins! You may as well hold tight and hope for the best, because you're in for the ride of your life. But how do you do it? Where do you start? Well, if you're willing to throw caution to the wind, ignore the bad press that some child actors have had in the media, jump in with your feet barely planted on the ground and eyes tightly shut—the truth be known—there's really no other way to do it.

– NOTES –

– NOTES –

6

2
What Makes A Child Actor?

What makes a child "right" for today's industry? That's easy. Today's child actor is talented, bright, outgoing, well-behaved, cheerful, animated, brave and—most importantly—willing to rise to the task of performing and to sparkle while he's doing it! He is aware and sensitive to his environment. If, by coincidence, this is the consummate description of your child, you've already mastered the most difficult part of the game. Congratulations!

We'll throw in a word of caution here, parents. You <u>must</u> be honest with yourself when assessing your child's attributes or electing to put him in show business. No matter how delightful he might be to you, he may not appear that way to others. Unfortunately, because of the strength of the parent-child bond, it is entirely possible to push a child into this industry against his will, even if he doesn't have talent or desire. If this scenario is true in your household, do your child a favor—close this book and call a shrink. Such parental prodding only ends up with disastrous consequences. Forcing any child to work against his will is abusive, no matter how you've rationalized it in your mind. If it's not okay for your child to be forced to be "forced" to work eight hours a day in a coal mine, it shouldn't be okay for him to be forced to work eight hours a day in front of a camera. Children want their parents' approval (that's what those temper tantrums are about, you know). So please, be thoughtful and loving parents: keep your sanity in check and refrain from coaxing a child against his will into a career in the industry. The pressures put on an unwilling child actor—no matter how talented you may think he is—are cruel, selfish and unjust. You can read in the tabloids just how far it will get you.

As parents, we must first and foremost be good, caring and responsible people in all matters concerning our children. We are their nurturers. Their protectors. Their guides. Their comforters. Whether a child is industry bound or not, he will be part of the generation that will carry on when we are gone. It is our responsibility to leave this world with citizens who are as balanced and sound as they were when we delivered them onto the planet.

All right then . . . you've assessed your child and he's truly talented, bright, outgoing, well-behaved, cheerful, animated and brave. (Just this once, we'll take your word for it.) So, how can you tell if he has any potential for acting? How do you know if he wants to be an actor? How about asking him?

It is likely that your child's behavior and personality already have given you an inkling of his potential acting ability. Most parents can recognize, just by looking at their children, whether or not they possess the qualities and disposition necessary for the industry. If you think your child might be a good actor, but you aren't sure if he has the requirements, here is a list of questions that will help you sort it out.

1. Is your child (A) outgoing and animated; or (B) quiet and shy?
2. Does he (A) say hello to someone when he's introduced; or (B) become distracted by things in his environment and doesn't realize someone is speaking to him?
3. Does he (A) respond when he's asked his name or age by someone he doesn't know; or (B) shrug his shoulders as if he no longer remembers what language he speaks?
4. Does he (A) love to sing and dance for you; or (B) think stuff like singing and dancing is stupid?
5. Does he (A) imitate what he sees on TV; or (B) forget what he was watching five minutes ago?

If you answered "A" to these questions, that's terrific! Most would-be industry children are little hams by nature, willing to show off at every opportunity.

Your child's ability to meet new people easily and to show off for them will be one of the most important factors in his career. We have to remember, nonetheless, that as responsible parents, we raise our children not to talk to strangers and the world of show business is contrary to this upbringing by 180 degrees. We therefore advise you to have continuing discussions with your child in this topic, especially after his career is launched. Make sure he knows the difference between meeting an unfamiliar casting person or working with a cast and crew of strangers, and speaking to strangers outside of these industry-type situations. The rules you teach him about talking to or going with strangers should remain the same as if he were not in the industry. The time for him to meet new people and make new adult friends is when you are present. When you're not present, he should avoid talking to or going anywhere with strangers.

Another important consideration, especially for infants, is your child's ability to separate easily from you. Will your infant go to a stranger without screaming when you hand him over? Casting directors won't give him a few days or even a few minutes to bond with the actor(s) playing his parent(s) during the audition. It's now or never when infants and the audition process are concerned. You will be in the room with your infant, but you will not be in front of the camera with him.

Separation from parents is even more important when your child is two or three years old. Casting directors prefer interviewing children over the age of two <u>without</u> their parents! If this shocks you, get over it, or get out of the business. It's a fact of life in this business. If it helps soothe your nerves, we will tell you to rest assured: nothing will happen to your child while out of your sight during the few minutes of an audition on a SAG sanctioned call. Once your child goes out on calls, you will realize that there is neither time, space, energy nor inclination towards lewd or permissive conduct during the casting process. This doesn't mean you shouldn't know where your child is at all times. A watchful eye is, after all, part of good parenting no matter what your child is doing. If, on the other hand, you're a nervous wreck while your child is away from you during an audition, there's only one place this nervousness will land: on your child.

Casting is a business. When you go on a call (or an "audition"), the person in charge of the call will simply come to the front of the room, holler out a list of names from the "sign-in sheet" and say to the kids whose names he just called, "Follow me." This group of kids then goes behind closed doors to be interviewed. It's exactly the same scenario when one child at a time is called. Audition schedules are usually packed tightly as a can of sardines because casting people strive to audition talent as quickly as can be managed. The young child who won't separate easily from his parent is going to experience difficulty in the audition process, not to mention his trauma if he actually winds up on a set where there are many new faces and distractions. Your child's sense of independence and his ability to separate from you willingly, should be thoughtfully considered before putting a very young child into the industry. If you have to peel him off you every time you introduce him to a new face, then pop the balloons, folks, 'cause the party's over!

Before you begin launching your child into the spotlight, we recommend sitting down and discussing with him your thoughts about his possible acting career. (If you don't know what that requires, you will by the time you finish reading this book.) Be specific when you talk to your child; be sure he understands exactly is be required of him. If your child is old enough—and that's usually after the age of four or five—it is imperative that he understands what is about to happen to him. A child actor's career should be something you and your child decide to do together. This endeavor requires both parent and child to be voluntary participants. After all, we're talking about his life, too! His feelings on the subject must be considered. If you approach the topic positively, your child will likely respond positively. You may even discover he likes the idea! (Remember, we said that "born in a trunk" children are rare, not extinct!)

Of course, if the only reason your child considers this endeavor is because you demand it, or if his response is less than enthusiastic, postpone this tête-à-tête for another time. Children's emotions are fickle: what he feels today he may not feel tomorrow. There may be days when—even if you offer him a trip to Disneyland to sweeten the deal—he would decline your offer. If, however, you elect to proceed with an unwilling child, you deserve what you get. It won't be pleasant.

HOW DO YOU KNOW IF HE'S READY?
Here are a couple of suggestions for testing the water. Prior to making your decision (and long after you've committed to it, too), watch programs together that focus on children your child's age. You'll find lots of child actors in television commercials too; in fact, in the beginning, your child will go out on more interviews for commercials than for any other medium. (TV series, feature films and movies of the week usually come after your child has done a few commercials.) When watching children, make comments to your child. For example, while viewing a pudding commercial featuring a five-year-old boy, you might say, "Wasn't he cute? I'll bet you could do that." If your child offers an affirmative response, ask him to say a couple lines about chocolate pudding; the lines do not have to be the same as those in the commercial. Let him make up something on his own. He may surprise you. If he can easily mimic what he hears, he's ready. If your child willingly performs for you upon request, he'll willingly do it for others, like casting directors, producers and directors. Of course, there's a big difference between performing for you and performing for someone outside of your family.

THE TEMPERAMENT

Once your child is going out on calls, keep in mind that he's just a kid. There will be days when he is "on" and days when, no matter what you promise him, he just won't do anything for anybody. Will the casting people understand? Of course they will. There will be other calls, other projects and there's no need to burn bridges with casting directors over an attitude caused by a missed nap. Keep in mind, however, there are <u>dozens</u> more kids just like yours lining up right outside the door, ready and willing to stand up and be counted. All the casting people have to do with a child who won't perform is say, "Next."

PRESSURE FROM THE PARENTS

Parents of newcomers often put too much pressure on themselves and their children on the first few auditions. (Shame on them!) If you can avoid the pressure while lapping up the excitement, you will be better off from the start, because there is no reward for pressure except for unnecessary stress on your child. Remember, the first call is only a first look. It simply means that the casting director has seen your child's picture (which your child's agent sent to him) and now, he would like to see for himself if your child has that "certain something" when they meet him in person.

There shouldn't be any pressure put on your child—no matter how important you may feel the audition is. You will never inspire in your child a positive attitude about acting if, every time he feels apprehensive, your disappointment in him is overwhelming. While your child may be exactly what the casting company is looking for (in your mind, anyway), so might fifty other kids! If your child has done his best on the audition, that is all you should expect from him. However, if he is having a rotten day and doesn't feel like performing, there shouldn't be hell to pay from you. Don't make your child perfect: this isn't a modeling call or a beauty pageant. This is reality and casting directors want <u>real</u> children. Child actors must be relaxed at all times in order to perform their best work. Whether your child is "on" or "off," your job is to keep him cool. The climate should always be cool, calm and collected. Your child is there to show off and shine.

Children are like little sponges. If yours thinks you're freaked out by all of this, how do you expect him to respond? Your child should feel that this new venture fits <u>into</u> his life, not replaces it! A little dirt on his face, messed-up hair, or a wrinkle on his shirt, can actually be a plus in keeping him relaxed enough to book a job. No, parents, we don't suggest you take your child on calls looking like he just rolled in the dirt (unless you're asked to by his agent or the casting director, of course). If he's a mess and there's honestly no time to clean him up before his audition, call his agent. She will advise you in a case like this. What we are trying to suggest is that you allow your child to be himself whenever possible.

– NOTES –

15

– NOTES –

3

Travel Time

Does distance have anything to do with a successful career in the business? It depends on the enthusiasm of the parent and the child when traveling a long distance to an audition or to work. Remember, however, that in the beginning, your enthusiasm will be at its highest. The first few calls will probably generate such excitement that you and your child would be willing to travel to Mars by hot-air balloon just to have a chance to audition. But, hold your horses. The first few audition calls for your child will more than likely be ones for which he won't be called back, let alone book the job. This can fray good-natured spirits. If you have to make a one- or two-hour commute to get to an audition that will last only a few minutes (once they take your child into the interview room), your child might be too uptight or fatigued to turn on the sparkle; it can be just as hard on you.

If your commute is long, you might seriously consider moving closer to the hub of the industry. However, that is a decision that should be born from your desire. You must always keep in mind that there are no guarantees in this business: nothing and no one can guarantee your child will ever be hired for one day of work. No matter how talented or well-suited you think he might be, it's possible he'll remain unemployed long enough to break you. Relocation is an idea that should be given careful consideration before you move your heart and homestead to a town just to be close to a business that may not want him.

We will tell you, nevertheless, that shortening the drive to and from the industry area can increase your child's chances positively. Ultimately, it will be less taxing on both of you. Remember, it's a two-way trip: once you arrive at the audition, you have to travel the same distance home. Our feeling is that a commute longer than one hour each way is too far. It takes too much of your time and, most importantly, your child's time. And what about car trouble? Something as simple as a flat tire can cause you to miss an audition if your commute is too long. And, during the school year, all interviews for children are scheduled after 3:00 P.M. and as late as 7:00 P.M. Going on a two-minute audition shouldn't take the better part of a day!

In California, the industry is located in and around the Hollywood-Los Angeles vicinities (spilling over into the San Fernando Valley as well). In New York, the industry can be found just about anywhere in Manhattan: uptown and downtown, east side and west side. The theater and film industries are bountiful there. In any state, the entertainment industry is usually located in the most densely populated area. If you moved to a secluded spot in the country to get away from the hustle of the city, odds are you're out of the mainstream of the industry in your area. While serene family communities are wonderful places to live and raise children, try making a two-hour commute during afternoon rush-hour traffic several times a week; you'll quickly see what we mean. We're not saying that a long commute can't be managed, only that it can tax the patience of any mild-mannered individual.

Distance becomes less of a problem once your child is established in the business. If he has a "name" in show business, it doesn't matter where you live because the industry will make special considerations for him. The audition process is regulated for kids who have well-established careers.

– NOTES –

4

Getting Started

Your child will need two legal documents in order to work in the industry: a work permit from the state where he resides and a Social Security Card. Obtaining a work permit may vary from state to state. Please check with the Department of Social Services in your area.

THE WORK PERMIT

Obtaining a work permit for your child is a simple task to accomplish. In California, you can get one at no cost from the Entertainment Work Permit Department found at the Department of Social Services in your area. Work permits are good for a six-month period and must be renewed every six months thereafter. Some parents make the mistake of waiting until the child books a job before obtaining a work permit. Don't be caught unprepared! It is entirely possible to find out your child has booked a job late Monday night and is expected to report to the set early Tuesday morning. Without an original copy of a work permit from your state, your child will not be allowed to work. You won't fool the production people or the social worker/studio teacher by saying you lost it or left it at home. For child actors, this is a hard and fast rule: without a work permit, your child will NOT be allowed to work! Work permits are required by the child's home state the child lives in and must be signed off by a social worker/studio teacher who is hired by the state to take care of your child's school and labor needs on the job. If your child is shooting out of town or in another state, the social worker/studio teacher from his home state must accompany him to the state in which the project is being filmed. Your child works under the laws of his home state, no matter where in the United States (or outside the United States) he is filming. For instance: If a child actor resides in California but is filming a project in Utah, the child and a California social worker/studio teacher will go to Utah to make the

STATE OF CALIFORNIA
Department of Industrial Relations
Division of Labor Standards Enforcement

ENTERTAINMENT WORK PERMIT
For Minors Under 18 Years of Age

...sent is herewith granted for the employment of

| Name | Age | Mo/Day/Yr of Birth |

Permanent Address (M)F Sex Weight Height

Temporary Address, if applicable Eye Color Hair Color

...in the entertainment industry for the period _____ to _____ unless sooner revoked. The above named minor will be employed NO LATER THAN 10 p.m.

Field of Employment	Type of Performance	City or Town	Theatre or Studio

Dated _____   State Labor Commissioner
By _____
District Office _____ VAN NUYS

OLSE 275 (Rev. 3-86)   ALTERATIONS WILL VOID THIS PERMIT

Sample work permit from the State of California.

RENEWAL

THIS IS NOT A PERMIT

STATE OF CALIFORNIA, Department of Industrial Relations, Division of Labor Standards Enforcement

APPLICATION FOR PERMISSION TO WORK IN THE ENTERTAINMENT INDUSTRY

PRINT LEGIBLY OR TYPE

Name of Child				Professional Name, if applicable		
Permanent Address	Number	Street	City	State	Zip Code	Home Phone Number ( )
School Attending						Grade
Mo/Day/Year of Birth / /	Sex M F	Weight	Height	Hair Color	Eye Color	Age

PROCEDURES FOR OBTAINING A WORK PERMIT:

1. Complete the information required above.
2. School authorities must complete the School Record section below designating satisfactory or unsatisfactory for each area requested.
3. During summer session, please enclose copy of recent report card.
4. Please submit renewal application with copy of previous permit.

STATEMENT OF PARENT OR GUARDIAN: It is my desire that an Entertainment Work Permit be issued to the above-named child. I will read the rules and regulations governing such employment and will cooperate to the best of my ability in safeguarding his or her educational, moral and physical interest.

Name of Parent or Guardian (print or type)			Signed	
Address of Parent or Guardian			Home Phone ( )	Day Time Phone ( )
Number	Street	City	State	Zip Code

SCHOOL RECORD

This section may only be completed by administrative staff for Jr. and Sr. High Schools (i.e., Principal, Vice Principal, Counselor, etc.). Individual teachers may complete for elementary schools.

Name of Minor		Birthdate	Grade
Attendance		Academic	Health

(State whether "Satisfactory" or "Unsatisfactory" for each). Grades must be "C" average or above

☐ I certify that the above-named minor meets the school district's requirements with respect to age, school record, attendance and health.

☐ Does not meet the district's requirements and permit should not be issued.

School Official	Date
School Address	School Telephone

AFFIX SCHOOL
SEAL

PLEASE SUBMIT ONE MONTH PRIOR TO EXPIRATION TO:

ENCLOSE A SELF ADDRESSED STAMPED ENVELOPE FOR THE RETURN OF YOUR PERMIT.

Entertainment Permit Section
Labor Standards Enforcement
5555 California Avenue #200
Bakersfield, CA 93309

Sample work permit renewal from the State of California.

movie, but both will work under the laws of the State of California. The child's parent or guardian must go as well, of course. The state makes no exceptions to this rule. Labor laws have been designed by each state to protect both child and parent.

The first time you apply for a work permit, if your child is school age, you will need to present a copy of his birth certificate as well as the name and address of the school he currently attends. If school is in session, it must acknowledge that your child's grades and conduct are in good standing. If school is not in session, you must present a copy of your child's last report card with your application. If your child is under five years of age, you will only need to present a copy of his birth certificate to obtain a work permit. After the initial permit is processed, the Department of Social Services will send you renewal forms by mail (two weeks before the current permit's expiration). Questions can be directed to the Department of Social Services.

You will retain an original copy to be presented to the social worker/studio teacher when your child works; if you leave the original at home, you will have to return home to get it. Another original is kept by the Department of Social Services.

SOCIAL SECURITY CARD

The purpose of the Social Security Card is to allow payment to be made to your child when he is working. It is state-regulated; payment to a minor cannot legally be made until the number is secured and given to the company that hired your child. It should be easy to obtain a Social Security Card because most children acquire Social Security numbers for their parents' income tax deduction purposes. A card can be obtained from the Department of Social Security either by mail or by visiting a local office. Call 800-772-1213 to have an application sent to you through the mail. You can also visit their web site at http://www.ssa.gov. The forms are available on-line. Two forms of identification are required, a birth certificate and any other form of identification with the information of your child's birth printed on it. If you want to visit the office in person, call the Social Security office to make sure the office still does business at the listed location; offices close on a regular basis and you may have to travel a long distance to find one that is open.

With the paperwork in order, the next task is getting an agent. Onward we forge.

Sample Social Security card.

– NOTES –

26

5
Finding An Agent

As most of you probably have heard, your child is going to need an agent. Not a business manager or a personal manager or a publicist. An agent. Managers and publicists are great—if and when you have something to manage and publicize. Once your child has started to attract bigger offers (and by that we mean six figures), it will be important for you to have people guiding your child in financial matters, negotiations, appropriateness of projects, and making sure that your child stays in the public's eye. These are the kinds of tasks that managers handle. Ultimately, they are a necessity for any successful actor's career. But, for now, remember this: managers don't send your child on interviews or book acting jobs. The only person who can send your child on calls or get him work in this business is an agent. Please don't fall prey to would-be managers or publicists. You will meet dozens of them, but be cautious. Most credible managers would not consider taking on a client without career momentum. If your child's career reaches the point where he needs a personal manager, you'll be approached by professionals and have a selection from which to choose. Until then, you are perfectly capable of managing your child's affairs on your own. Until your child is earning enough of it to afford the luxury of a manager or publicist, there is no need to pay another 10 percent to 20 percent of your child's income to someone who is just along for the ride. Right now, what you need is an AGENT!

FACTS ABOUT TALENT AGENCIES
The following information is distributed by the Los Angeles Office of the Consumer Protection Division of the Federal Trade Commission:

Question: What is the difference between a legitimate talent agency and one whose purpose is to separate you from your money?
Answer: The legitimate talent agency does not charge a fee payable in advance for registering you, for resumes, for public relations services, for screen tests, for photographs, for acting lessons, or for many other services used to separate you from your money. If you are signed as a client by a legitimate talent agency, you will pay such agency nothing until you work and then ten percent ("commission") of your earnings as a performer—but nothing in advance. Legitimate talent agencies normally do not advertise for clients in newspaper classified columns nor do they solicit through the mail.

Are legitimate talent agencies licensed by the State of California?
Yes. Such talent agencies are licensed by the State as Talent Agents and most established agencies in the motion picture and television film field are also franchised by

the Screen Actors Guild. You should be extremely careful of any talent agency not licensed by the State.

What about personal managers and business managers?

There are well established firms in the business of personal management and business management but such firms in the main handle established artists and they do not advertise for newcomers, nor promise employment.

The above information is specific to the State of California, but use this criteria before signing an agency contract or accepting verbal representation in any State.

SCHEDULE OF FEES

THE MAXIMUM RATE OF FEES DUE THIS TALENT AGENCY FOR SERVICES RENDERED TO THE ARTIST IS TEN PER CENT (10%) OF THE TOTAL EARNINGS PAID TO THE ARTIST MANAGED BY THIS TALENT AGENCY.

"IN THE EVENT THAT A TALENT AGENCY SHALL COLLECT FROM AN ARTIST A FEE OR EXPENSES FOR OBTAINING EMPLOYMENT FOR THE ARTIST AND THE ARTIST SHALL FAIL TO PROCURE SUCH EMPLOYMENT, OR THE ARTIST SHALL FAIL TO BE PAID FOR SUCH EMPLOYMENT, SUCH TALENT AGENCY SHALL, UPON DEMAND THEREFOR, REPAY TO THE ARTIST THE FEE AND EXPENSES SO COLLECTED. UNLESS REPAYMENT THEREOF IS MADE WITHIN FORTH-EIGHT (48) HOURS AFTER DEMAND THEREFOR. THE TALENT AGENCY SHALL PAY TO THE ARTIST AN ADDITIONAL SUM EQUAL TO THE AMOUNT OF THE FEE."
(SECTION 1700.40, CALIFORNIA LABOR CODE)

"IF ANY CONTROVERSY ARISES BETWEEN THE PARTIES, INCLUDING ONE AS TO LIABILITY FOR THE PAYMENT OF FEES, THE PARTIES INVOLVED SHALL REFER THE MATTER IN DISPUTE TO THE LABOR COMMISSIONER FOR HEARING AND DETERMINATION AS PROVIDED IN SECTION 1700.44, LABOR CODE, UNLESS SUCH CONTROVERSY CAN BE HANDLED IN ACCORDANCE WITH THE PROVISIONS OF SECTION 1700.45 OF THE LABOR CODE."
(SECTION 12003.5 CALIFORNIA ADMINISTRATIVE CODE)

THIS IS TO CERTIFY THAT THE above schedule of fees has been filed with the Labor Commissioner of the State of California. NO FEES COLLECTED SHALL BE IN EXCESS OF THE FEES SCHEDULED HEREON.

AUG 2 3 1985
Date

State Labor Commissioner

POST IN A CONSPICUOUS PLACE
California
Department of Industrial Relations
DIVISION OF LABOR STANDARDS ENFORCEMENT

DLSE 314 (New 11/78)

WHAT MAKES A GOOD AGENT?

First, ask yourself, how does a person become an agent? There are probably as many reasons as there are agents, however, agents are often one-time performers who possess an excellent sense for business. From Broadway to Hollywood, there are countless former actors and actresses who are now doing for other people what was once done for them. Who would know more about this business than a person who was once in it? It takes a bountiful love for the arts to be involved in the pursuit of other people's success and happiness. You will find that most agents who represent children are dedicated and talented. They will usually tell you they love their work. How many people can claim that about their jobs? Not many, we'll tell you right now. The agent's job is to find out about potential acting jobs and to send actors out on interviews.

If the job is offered, the agent negotiates the terms of the deal. Most agents will represent some children with recognizable names or faces. If they don't, that agency may not be a good children's agency and you might continue your search. You should also note that most agencies don't represent children exclusively, but may have a children's department within it. There are also selective agencies that only represent a select group of child actors. (Asking who an agency represents is not unreasonable.) For the most part, as long as an agency is franchised with the Screen Actors Guild and gets the daily breakdowns for projects, it is suitable enough to represent your child.

The relationship with your child's agent is the most important one you will have in connection with your child's career (outside of his relationship with you, of course).

WHERE DO YOU FIND THE MOST AGENTS
FROM WHICH TO CHOOSE?

Where do you go for the best chance of success? Hollywood! (The second-best location is New York. Check the list we have provided at the back of this book.) Agencies in Hollywood and New York are contacted everyday by hopeful parents from all over the country who seek representation for their child. These parents are willing to pack up and move—lock, stock and barrel—from Two Ticket Tennessee, for the chance of launching their child in the entertainment industry. Moving from another state with the sole purpose of putting your child in the business should <u>not</u> be a whimsical action. Even if your child eventually enjoys a successful career, he's not going to get there overnight. And, you, his parents, are limited by law to the actual amount of his money you can spend. (See Chapter Sixteen, "Managing Your Child's Money.") Unless you have a job that supports the family and allows you to take your child on calls, you're going to be in desperate straits from the start! If taking your child on calls doesn't fit easily into your daily schedule, reconsider this whole venture, because, my, oh my, the pressure is unbelievable. If, however, someone in the family has been transferred to a show business mecca and you have a child who is interested in working in the industry, pick up the phone and start soliciting representation. It's possible to set up interviews with agents if you are planning on relocating to a show business area. (The process of getting representation is the same, no matter where you live.)

HOW DO YOU GET IN TOUCH WITH AN AGENT?

If you don't already have an agent or agency in mind, or you haven't a clue where to begin, it's as simple as placing a call or writing a letter to one of the agents on the list provided at the back of this book. You could also call the Screen Actors Guild (SAG) in Los Angeles or New York if you want a more current list of SAG-franchised talent agencies. Agency information changes: Sometimes it's the address and phone number; other times it's the type of talent an agency represents. An agency may not represent children this month, but may change its mind next month and add a children's department. When you call SAG, ask for a current list of theatrical agencies. They will happily send it out to you. It is also available on-line at http://www.sag.com/agentlist.html.

The next step is a snap: Starting at the top of the agency list for your area, call the first name you see listed. You might as well start with the A's and work your way down. You could, of course, pre-pare your own list from SAG. Maybe you have a formula or lucky letter or you just have a "feeling" about a particular agency. Go with that. For those of you who live in an area where the industry is less visible, the list of agents to choose from might only consist of a few names. Get individual agent names, if possible. Start with your area, and if need be, move on to the next area closest to yours. When you contact them, ask if they represent children.

While this initial step may seem hard, it will pale by comparison to the task of maintaining your child in the business once he starts going out on calls and—heaven help you!—he is actually working. But, we're getting ahead of ourselves. Let's stay focused on the subject. To secure representation from an agent, you must first contact one. There are those of you who might feel more comfortable using the postal system. Phone calls are quicker, but the mail is cheaper and you can do mass solicitations via the post. (Phone calls are placed one at a time, and sometimes require several return calls before reaching someone helpful.)

SECURING REPRESENTATION
THROUGH THE MAIL

To illustrate what NOT to do, we have included some actual letters sent to agencies from parents who were seeking representation for their children. Parents will say some of the silliest things, especially when seeking representation for tiny tots!

"Dear Agency:
Here is a picture and resume of my daughter, Sharon. Sharon is an outgoing child who enjoys being in front of the camera. Sharon has been a consistent

participant and winner of many beauty pageants due to her expressive facial features.
Thank you for your time and I look forward to having the opportunity to meet with you regarding Sharon's involvement with your agency."

This letter is from the mother of a three-and-a-half-_month_-old infant! The girl can't even talk yet and Mom's got her cast as a natural in front of the camera. (She means a still camera, of course.) This young child has no credits in front of a _movie_ camera. One wonders how the mother knows that Sharon's cute smile isn't caused by a little gas.

"Dear Agency:
My six-year-old has the greatest personality. Wait until you see

him. I know he'll make it in
Show Biz."

Is she kidding? "Wait until you see him?" When does she think that's going to happen? She doesn't even know if the agency handles children or is taking on any new clients.

"Dear Agency:
Everywhere I go, people are
always stopping me and telling
me my baby should be in commercials. I'm just a regular Mom,
but if perfect strangers are
telling me this, maybe I should
think about putting him in the
movies.
With feedback like this, I know
he'll be great for your agency!"

Agents get dozens of letters like these on a daily basis. Your purpose in the first communiqué is to learn if the agency is taking on any new clients. Then, give the agency the necessary information, letting it or the agent know your child is available for representation. You do not need to hard-sell your child.

If you're going to send a letter to an agent rather than call, it should follow the line of the sample below:

"Dear Agency:
I am looking for representation
for my two-year-old son, Raymond
(born 2/15/91). Raymond is 38
inches tall, weighs 35 pounds,
has brown hair and brown eyes
and is very friendly and outgoing.

I have enclosed a picture for your consideration and look forward to your response. I can be reached at (101) 555-5555."

Don't forget to include pertinent information on your child: date of birth; height; weight; clothing size; eye color; hair color; and any special talents (e.g., sports, musical talents, dancing, juggling).

This information is sufficient to get the ball rolling—if the agency is looking for new clients. If they are <u>not</u> in the market for new faces, don't discount them permanently. Try them again in a few months if you haven't secured representation elsewhere. If you include a self-addressed, stamped envelope, the agency will return your child's photo if it declines to represent him. Whatever you do, hold onto the agency's name, address and phone number for future reference.

SECURING REPRESENTATION OVER THE PHONE

The list of agents to contact by phone is the same list you use to reach them by letter. While calling can be ten times more intimidating than sending a letter, it is faster and is often more efficient, producing a better chance for an interview with the agent or a request to forward pictures because you have made contact with a real person.

The method for securing representation over the phone is as follows: Pick up the phone; dial a number. When the phone is answered, you begin: "Hello, my name is Mrs./Mr. so-and-so and I'm looking for theatrical and commercial representation for my *(blank)*-year-old daughter/son." If the agency is interested in taking on a new client, the person on the phone may ask you some basic questions about your child, such as how did you decide to call her, or why you want to get your child in show busi-

Snapshots of children being themselves is the type to send to an agent.

ness. On the other hand, she may simply ask you to forward your child's picture for consideration. If the agent is not taking on new child talent, she will let you know immediately and you should proceed to the next agency on the list. When you contact an agency that is considering new talent (and you will), the agency may set up an appointment for you and

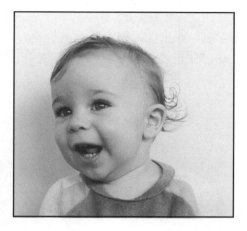

your child to meet the children's agent, or, more than likely, you may be asked to send in your child's snapshot so she can get a "first look" at this potential client before scheduling an interview. Please remember, a <u>regular</u> family snap will do. Pick a photo that clearly represents your child. Something natural. You may have expensive, beautiful studio portraits, or a snap from a local pageant or modeling call, but those kinds of photos are not the ticket here. Remember: natural, a photo showing your child's personality, one that reflects his inner self.

Can you hand-deliver this picture to the agency? Certainly. Theatrical agencies are not closed to the general public the way movie studios and casting companies are. Deliveries in person will give you a peek into an area that, until this point, has scared the wits out of you. After the agent receives the photo (by mail or by hand), if she has any interest, she will call you to set up an appointment for an interview with your child so she can determine if his personality and temperament are suited for this business, as well as the agency's needs. For instance, if your child is seven years old and the agency you've contacted has an abundance of seven-year-olds, it, more than likely, will pass on meeting your child for obvious reasons. Don't be discouraged, merely proceed to the next agency.

Even if you're soliciting representation from another state, there is no need to say anything more

When sending a photo to an agent, it should look natural.
Remember to put your child's name, date of birth, height, weight and phone number on the back of the photo.

than what is outlined above. For example, if you live in Tucson, Arizona, but are planning a visit to Hollywood, California, try to set up appointments with agencies in Hollywood, coinciding with the dates of your trip. While in the agent's office, you then could explain that you are relocating to Los Angeles at a future date and that you are taking the opportunity to meet with her now and

Studio snapshots are great if they don't look too stiff or posed. When you send a studio snapshot to an agent, include candid photos as well.

introduce her to your child (children). More than likely, if the agent is interested in your child, she will tell you to call her after you've relocated. The fact that she has invited you to contact her again is a definite positive! (Agents have no problem saying "No, thanks" to the children they don't want to interview or represent. The ability to pass out "turn-downs" is some-

thing agents must do in their line of work. On the other hand, if the agent thinks your child is the find of the century, she'll let you know that, too.) She'll want to know when you'll be in town permanently so that she can start sending your child out on calls. She'll also want you to set up a session for professional photos, secure work permits and social security numbers, etc.

MEETING THE AGENT

As nervous as you may be with this process, we advise you to meet with more than one agency (in the cities where there are several available to you). There's no need to inform each agent of the other agents you are meeting; they won't care and it makes you look like an amateur. If someone is interested in representing your child, but you have

agencies. A few will do nicely and give you something to choose from.

Finding representation is the single most uncomplicated task you will master with this new venture, so try not complicate it by overextending yourself.

If there are <u>two</u> parents in the home, both should be present at the initial interview with the agent. For the most part, agents like to study what comes with the package (the package being your child). Once you arrive at the agent's office, if the agency is looking for your child's type, age, etc., and if you can get your child to say his name, age and maybe even smile while doing it, the agent will probably be willing to give him a try. The agent/actor relationship is <u>not</u> a complicated one; you're selling and they're buying. It's that simple. Be honest with the agent about your child's credits.

appointments with other agents, you simply say, "May I let you know at such-and-such a date. We have a few more people to meet." The agent, most likely, will be agreeable, because you have been honest. You should limit the number of agencies you visit—you should not be talking with <u>dozens</u> of

No need to fudge what you think are credits. The agent knows she is interviewing a newcomer; a lack of professional credits is what she is expecting. If you lie about this, you will be discovered sooner or later.

If your child has what the agent is looking for, he'll get representation.

By the way, if you know an agent or someone recommends an agent to you, the interview process remains pretty much the same. Like any other business, there are few free lunches. (You may get an appointment a little faster or you may skip sending photos for review, but agents, as a rule, do not handle children as a favor to a friend unless that child has a special quality.)

A word of caution, parents. We're talking about "actor" agents here, not "extra" agents. There is a huge difference. The old saying, "Once an extra, always an extra," wasn't created from thin air. Registering your child with the Screen Extras Guild (SEG) is not the same as getting your child into the Screen Actors Guild (SAG). Extras are never treated as well as actors, even if they're SEG members. If an actor works three SEG jobs, he can then

IF YOUR CHILD IS AN INFANT

Let's try to be grown up about this. When trying to get representation for an infant, don't be goofy. Agents are not interested in knowing if the baby says "da" or "goo goo!" If your child has an outgoing personality and is not scared of strangers, sights and/or noises, it's a safe bet that he'll have

join SAG. However, he will not have earned enough money from all three jobs to pay for joining . . . and, his SEG credits won't count as SAG credits. We don't recommend anyone doing extra work after becoming a member of SAG.

What does an agent look for in a child actor? That's easy . . . they look for SPARKLE . . . and lots of it!

a good chance getting representation. (You will notice we don't mention a child's attractiveness; the truth is: beauty isn't a huge criteria when it comes to actors.) By outgoing personality, do we mean your child should be "on" all the time? Of course, not. All children experience disposition changes, especially children between infancy and three years. As most of you already know, one day your little one may be agreeable and cooperative and the next day, you may find him cantankerous and overly-sensitive. No child is perfect all the time and it is unreasonable for any parent to demand this from a wee one. In fact, the word "perfect" probably should be excised from the English language when characterizing human beings; there aren't any "perfect" people on this planet. It's even more absurd to describe children this way. Children are children and perfection is not expected of them from anyone in this business. This is one of the reasons why twins are often cast to play a single part, es-

  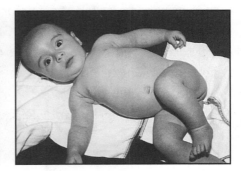

pecially if the role is large and the age requirement is young. If one twin is having a bad day, just bring in the other twin and shooting continues.

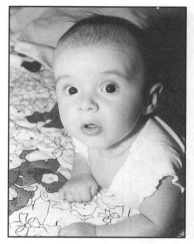

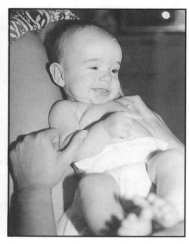

There are also projects that require the use of "back-up" kids, who are substitute actors hired to fill in for (or "back up") young actors. If a child under five is cast as the principal actor in a project, a back-up actor (sometimes two or more) will also be on call for that day of shooting. Should the prin-

cipal actor be unwilling to perform on that day, the director will request one of the back-up actors to fill in (or, ask for the second or third, etc.) until he gets a performance from one of the child actors. The child who winds up on film is the one who will become the principal player; he will receive the principal dollars and residuals, even if your child was originally booked as the principal. Don't flip out about this! Most often, the actor hired as the principal player, is the one who ends up on film.

WHAT ABOUT
BEAUTY PAGEANTS?

In some parts of the country, beauty pageants are the only venue to exposure for your child. There is little value in telling an agency about the countless beauty pageants and contests your child has won. Beauty pageants are a good indicator for judging your child's ability to

CARLEE BATES

stand in front of people (and will give you a positive answer to the question, "How cute is your child?"), the television and motion picture businesses are looking for all types of children, not beauty pageant winners and models. In fact, some of the most successful children in the industry probably couldn't win a beauty contest. The point is, don't start off on the wrong foot. Once you're face-to-face with the agent, you can mention about your child whatever you think is necessary, because the agent will have your child right there and will be able to judge for herself whether your child's talents are apparent.

We're not saying you should totally discount your child's crowns and ribbons, after all, it's fun to show off your child at family gatherings. However, the only beauty pageant that can be helpful to a child is a national one—and not everybody can be Miss Teenage America. When considering pageants for your child, remember that contestants usually are required to maintain mechanical or formal posture (even in the talent segment of a pageant). This "stiff" body language couldn't be more

Savannah Houser

contrary to that required by young actors in the entertainment industry. A child needs to be relaxed every time he goes on a call. However, a pageant or two won't hurt. They are a wonderful way to test the waters for your child's independence and they can be fun, too. Keep your sense of humor and remember the value, or lack thereof, of using these events as credits.

As mentioned, beauty pageants don't necessarily lead to careers in television and motion pictures but they sometimes lead to modeling careers. And a

good career in modeling can most certainly lead to a career in the industry.

THE AGENT IS LOOKING FOR WHAT KIND OF KIDS AGAIN?

The people who hire child actors look for that special face—not necessarily a beautiful one—but one with a quality that jumps out at you. A "sparkle!" There's that word again. Sparkle. It's not to be confused with a good personality (which is a combination of charm and wit); sparkle is something that comes from within. Its effect on an agent or a casting director is unbeatable. Who can resist a sparkling personality?

A sparkling personality is what sets one child apart from the rest. It's his sense of ease in the company of, or when engaged in conversation with adults. It's his ability to take direction, to be a good listener and to spread a joyful spirit.

– NOTES –

50

6

Who's In The Hot Seat?

When you meet an agent, remember: your child is the focus of the interview. You are of secondary interest and only if the agent decides she wants to represent him. When you interview with an agent, let your child do the talking. Sometimes parents feel they should be running the show. But, the parent is not the _actor_ in the family. The agent is most interested in seeing what your child, not you, has to offer. Your concerns of dominating the conversation or distracting the agent with endless questions about her experience or the agency's background, is a waste of everyone's time. If the agent is franchised with SAG, licensed by the state, has an office and clients, trust that she's a bona fide theatrical agent. It's appropriate to ask what other kids the agent/agency represents. But, that's it. If you have questions about the legitimacy of the agent, call SAG, which will fairly and honestly tell you about the quality and/or track record of that particular agent/agency.

Remember, the most important people in your child's career are you and his agent! And the first and most important step is for you to find your child the right person to represent him, someone

Height: 4' • Hair: Black • Eyes: Dk. Brown • Date of Birth: 10-31-87 • Dress: 7/8 • Shoe: 1

who is confident in every aspect of your child's abilities and his physical makeup.

Once you have secured representation and your child is sent out on calls, you'll eventually run into parents of other children the agency represents. Talking to other parents is a good way to learn more about a particular agent. Of course, when speaking with parents of other industry children, you may encounter one who is biased. This may be good or bad. A parent may be disgruntled with a particular agent because he feels his potential "star" isn't sent on enough auditions. Take a good look at his child: perhaps it's obvious why that child's career lacks activity! However, you're just as likely to meet a parent who can't say enough marvelous things about the agent who represents his little one. Exchanging stories with other parents can be fun, but don't let the sinister head of rivalry overcome you. Yes, you will meet children who go out three times more often than your child. There are countless reasons for this. Remember: type, credits, ability, personality, are factors in any child's career. Be patient. You're a newcomer and there's a lot to learn. Your turn will come. Put your child's best foot (and personality) forward. Have faith in the agent and your child. No actor's career is launched overnight. We can't say this often enough.

SEPARATION FROM MOM AND DAD

Besides sparkle and personality, a child's independence is an important factor for the agent to consider. Does your child separate from you easily and happily? This often is a question that parents can't answer. After all, how often do you test it in real life? You usually go where ever your child goes, except for school.

A mother of three-year-old triplets interviewed with an agent interested in representing her children. She told the agent that she <u>never</u> let her children out of her sight. (She was probably trying to represent herself as a responsible parent.) The overly-protective mother would not allow the agent to interview her triplets without her. However, the children would not have separated easily in any case. There was nothing left for the agent to do but inform the mother that the business has no room for clinging children or over-anxious parents!

This mother, and others like her, will have a difficult time in the industry if they continue to guide their children toward careers in show business. Kids with sparkle and personality are in abundance all over the country and non-separating children or their controlling parents are not needed in the business. You can always test the water again when the child is a little older. Children go through phases and being clingy today does not necessarily mean he'll be clingy six months from now.

BAD PRESS
We hear a lot of negative things in the press today and child actors are not spared.

We're often deluged with information from well-meaning friends and family members relaying media stories about corrupted or exploited children from the entertainment industry. Unfortunately, it sometimes happens, but it is rarer than you think. The press and some parents may be tempted to blame the actor's agent or the entertainment industry for the child's ruined career. But, most often, a child's career in the industry is ruined by his parents. If you are afraid of allowing your child to be himself with an agent or casting director, you

FILM ARTISTS ASSOCIATES
7080 HOLLYWOOD BOULEVARD • SUITE 1118
HOLLYWOOD, CALIFORNIA 90028 • (213) 463-1010

KRYSTIN ALEXIS

DATE OF BIRTH: 7-4-91

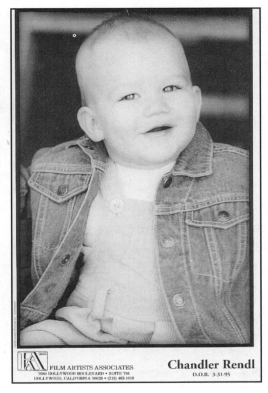

FILM ARTISTS ASSOCIATES
7080 HOLLYWOOD BOULEVARD • SUITE 704
HOLLYWOOD, CALIFORNIA 90028 • (213) 463-1010

Chandler Rendl

D.O.B. 3-31-95

should put this fear to rest or stop pursuing a career for your child. Agents and casting directors are reputable people; their single objective is making money. They rely on their reputations and hard work to keep them untarnished. If you feel the business is riddled with sexual deviants, rethink this adventure for you and your child.

When you are soliciting representation from an agency that is franchised and licensed agency, you know that its agents will behave professionally. Any other kind of behavior will cause an agent to lose her license with SAG, which is the guardian for all theatrical talent agents and their clients.

WHAT SHOULD YOUR CHILD WEAR TO MEET THE AGENT?

Any type of comfortable clothing that represents what your child looks like when he is the most re-laxed and feeling like himself is the best. Jeans and T-shirts for boys and girls alike are good; if it's summertime and the weather is warm, shorts and a tank top are fine. Under no circumstances should you dress your child in elaborate clothing—no suits or party dresses! (Dress clothes show the agent that you think you're entering another beauty contest; the fact is, the entertainment business is anything but a beauty contest. Perfect looks, grace and poise will only translate to stiff and uncomfortable in the eyes of an agent.) How a child is dressed often has a positive effect on his personality. And, once your child goes out on calls, casting director can be specific as to what clothing they want your child to wear to the audition. For example, casting agents may request your child wear pajamas for a certain audition. Why? Because kids don't always look the same when dressed in the same clothes. If you dress your child in a suit and tie when they want to see him in Doctor Dentons and slippers, your child will reflect a small business man instead of a young kid. Casual clothing on your child will automatically make him feel more relaxed and is the wardrobe required for most interviews.

– NOTES –

7
How Do You Cope With Nervousness?

You may be nervous before your first meeting with an agent. Quite honestly, sometimes a butterfly or two in the pit of one's stomach can be very helpful; keeping you alert and on your toes. But be careful not to turn that excitement into dread or anxiety, especially concerning your child. Let him breathe. All he needs to know about the interview is that he is going to meet someone who may represent him as an actor. If your child is very young, you can tell him he's going to meet a new friend or a friend of Mommy's. Whatever you say, make sure he understands that the meeting is something fun and no big deal. After all, if your child feels your pressure or anxiousness and the meeting doesn't go well, he's likely to feel he's disappointed you.

If you are consistently hovering over your child, your behavior can make both of you too nervous. The message you'll send to him will be: "This is something very important and if I leave it up to you, I know you're going to screw it up!" Your child will have more confidence in himself if you give him some breathing room. To quote Cole Porter: "Accentuate the positive. Depreciate the negative."

Do tell your child that he looks fabulous, that he should be himself. Tell him he can say whatever he wants but to listen when another person is speaking.

Let him know he can ask questions; he may want information on topics you had no idea he was thinking about!

Independence is a crucial ingredient of a flourishing child actor's career. For example, when your child is booked for an interview, he is interviewed <u>alone</u>; or, if your child gets a callback, he goes <u>alone</u>, or, when your child books a job, he is filmed <u>alone</u>! Mom and Dad are not permitted in the casting offices with their children; they are restricted to the outer waiting room. The scenario is only slightly better when your child is filming on the set. You are not permitted in front of the camera with your child, but you are somewhere on the sidelines and your child is in full view. On the set, your job is simple: keep an eye on your child, stay out of the way and be ready if you're needed. If you're lucky, you'll be able to watch the action on a monitor.

When your child is filming, a social worker/studio teacher is assigned to take care of his physical and legal needs. The social worker knows the state laws and the industry rules, for example, when he needs a break, when he needs water, etc. Every issue concerning your child is addressed and handled appropriately. As the parent, you will be nearby. A child can become tense when scrutinized too closely by someone he knows. Yes, Mom and Dad, this means you!

When your child interviews with an agent, parents, take a seat in the back and let your kid do his thing! He can handle it; if he can't, you've made a mistake bringing him this far. The best for him way to gain experience is to allow for a margin of error. As long as his attitude and behavior are correct, he'll survive.

It will only take a short time for an agent to see if your child can converse easily, read (if he is old enough) and show off his sparkling personality. Remember the agent is not looking for perfection, but for reality. A child comfortable with himself is best off left to his own devices.

The agent may ask your child to perform. She may have him read lines (also called "sides") if he is of reading age. If he is still very young, he may be asked to show happiness, sadness, fright or surprise. If he is willing to try, the agent will be able to judge how well he takes direction. Ultimately, the agent will know within minutes whether your child is focused enough for this business.

HOW FAST DOES IT HAPPEN?

It doesn't happen overnight. There will be sufficient time for your child to adjust to the demands made on him—if you give him the right kind of support and show your enthusiasm when helping him acquire the necessary skills. Just like adult actors, child actors don't start at the top! Most likely, your child will being with interviews for commercials; eventually, he will go out for theatrical jobs. Remember, your child learned to <u>crawl</u> before he learned to <u>walk</u>!

Parents, please be aware that agents don't make casting decisions! Casting directors determine whether or not your child will be seen on a particular call. The agent's job is to submit your child's name and picture for the casting director's consideration.

Once your child starts going on calls, don't make

the mistake of comparing other children to yours even if another child is represented by your child's agency. You will meet children who seem to be going out on twice as many interviews as yours, but don't get bent out of shape. It's not favoritism. There may be many reasons why your child was not asked to a particular call, but it's not because your agent likes the other kid better than yours. It's nothing personal. Your child's turn will come.

You may feel your child has every asset that any casting person could want, but every parent feels that way about his child! Casting people can be general or <u>very</u> <u>specific</u> about kids they want to see. Just make sure your child is ready when the agent calls; until that time, relax! If you don't, you might ruin everything, including your child's chances at any kind of career.

NOW THAT YOUR CHILD HAS AN AGENT

Once your child has secured representation, feel free to ask his agent what you need to know about how representation works, what the commissions are, about your child's talent and of course, any questions you have about the entertainment industry in general.

Although the agent will spend most of the time interviewing your child, the agent is also interested in speaking with you—after she has made some basic decisions about your child, that is. In fact, she has decided she is interested in handling him, she will have a lengthy conversation with you. Enjoy it . . . long conversations with agents are few and far between! More than likely, the agent will even be interrupted during your interview by phone calls concerning her other clients and when the agent says "Time's up," she means just that. Don't let this bother you. It's annoying that she may not give you her total attention, but it comes with the territory. When it's your turn to call her, you know she'll speak to you, even if she's in a meeting with someone else.

Once your child has secured an agent, be sure to ask if she has a problem with you calling in to see what's going on. This is particularly important when things are slow in this business. If you've been waiting for the phone to ring, or you just want to make sure the agency hasn't dumped your child (the most common fear of any actor, no matter his age) the agent should be willing to take your call and fill you in as to what's been going on. You can't imagine how good it feels to have an explanation for the lack of activity. A good agent is compassionate and if your child has not been busy, there's a good chance the agent hasn't been busy,

either. There are also times when it's busy for one age group and not for another. Sooner or later, though, everyone gets his turn.

If your child's agent is sending him out on calls, she's doing her part in building his career. The more people your child meets in this business, the greater his chances of working. The first job for any new actor, young or old, is the hardest to land and in order to succeed at that task, you need an agent who can get you out on as many calls as possible.

It's important to remember that the agent wants your child to work—as do you and your child. After all, agents are paid strictly on commission; they receive a standard ten percent, no matter the agent or the agency's size. If an agency's clients aren't working, the agency isn't making money: ten percent of nothing is nothing.

DO YOU HAVE TO SIGN A CONTRACT WITH THE AGENCY?

Usually, an agent will test the water by giving your child a three-month trial period (without a contract) for commercial and theatrical representation. Whether or not the relationship continues after this trial period often depends on the attitude of the parents and their child actor. However, some of the larger agencies may ask you to sign a formal one-year contract, giving them a second option for another one-year period. If you like the agent/agency, go ahead and sign; if they don't find work for your child within ninety days, by law, the contract is invalid and you're free to move on. You should note, however, that three months isn't a long enough period to determine whether or not your child will ever work in the industry. If the agent sends your child out on many calls, there's no need to change agencies. The agent is doing her job; it's not likely there's another agent out there who can make it happen any faster.

When it comes to representing children, most agencies will take on a new face no matter how old the child is. If your child has that extra something, they'll be interested in handling him. The demand for eight-year-olds is the same this year as it was last, and will remain the same next year. Children rarely play anything but themselves.

HOW MANY HOURS A DAY CAN A CHILD WORK?

SAG outlines the time allotted each day for children's work hours as defined by the Labor Board of each state. In California, schedules are divided by age group, as follows:

Younger than six years of age—six hours (excluding meal periods but including school time, if school is in session);

Six to Nine years of age—eight hours (excluding meal periods but including school time, if school is in session);

Nine to sixteen years of age—nine hours (excluding meal periods but including school time, if school is in session);

Sixteen to Eighteen years of age—ten hours (excluding meal periods but including school time, if school is in session).

Although it has happened, it's unusual for a child be asked to work longer hours than SAG's guidelines. Yes, it's true that sometimes a small six-year-old is cast in the role of a four-year-old, but it's not the rule of thumb. Don't concern yourself with this as, usually, a child plays his actual age.

Summary of California Child Labor Laws, Current as of May 1, 1996

Age	Max. Work Time	Education	Rest & Recreation	Meal Period	Total Time at Location
15 Days to 5+ mos	20 min (Max. 100 ft. candle light, 30 sec. exposure)			$\frac{1}{2}$ hr	2 $\frac{1}{2}$ hrs
6 mo to 1+ yr	2 hrs	0	2 hrs	$\frac{1}{2}$ hr	4 $\frac{1}{2}$ hrs
2 yrs to 5+ yrs	3 hrs	(3 hrs. Education and R & R)		$\frac{1}{2}$ hr	6 $\frac{1}{2}$ hrs
6 yrs to 8+ yrs	4 hrs	3 hrs	1 hr	$\frac{1}{2}$ hr	8 $\frac{1}{2}$ hrs
Non-school days	6 hrs	0	1 hr	$\frac{1}{2}$ hr	8 $\frac{1}{2}$ hrs
9 yrs to 15+ yrs	5 hrs	3 hrs	1 hr	$\frac{1}{2}$ hr	9 $\frac{1}{2}$ hrs
Non-school days	7 hrs	0	1 hr	$\frac{1}{2}$ hr	9 $\frac{1}{2}$ hrs
16 yrs to 17+ yrs	6 hrs	3 hrs	1 hr	$\frac{1}{2}$ hr	10 $\frac{1}{2}$ hrs
Non-school days	8 hrs	0	1 hr	$\frac{1}{2}$ hr	10 $\frac{1}{2}$ hrs

IS THERE SUCH A THING AS TOO TALL OR TOO SMALL?

A talented child probably can survive being any height. However, sometimes a child who is tall for his age may not be right for commercials since most kids selected are average in height or smaller than average. In the long run, smaller children usually have more longevity in this business than do taller children. Although children usually fit the age range requested by casting, there are six- and seven-year-old children who will be cast to play three-, four- and five-year-old kids. Why? Because a six-year-old can work a full eight-hour day whereas a child under six is limited to a six-hour day. Thus, the six-year-old who can play a four-year-old will save the production company time and money. Although it's done rarely, every now and then, a child who is large for his age will be cast in a part older than his years. This is rare and nothing is chiseled in stone in this industry. But, if your child is talented, his height, age, weight, etc., will have little bearing on his success.

WHAT'S CONSIDERED TO BE A "HAPPENING" CAREER?

A child actor with a "happening" career is one who goes out on a consistent basis, is called back often and books one out of every ten or fifteen calls, for commercials, television or motion pictures. An extremely "happening" career is when a child is booking one out of every <u>eight</u> or <u>ten</u> calls. How many kids in the business today are doing that well? According to SAG, over 80 percent of its members (about 84,000) earned $10,000 or <u>less</u> in 1996, the majority of SAG members (adults and children) are unemployed as performers on any given day.

"What!" you exclaim with a gasp. "Eighty percent of <u>all</u> SAG actors, adults and children, make $10,000 a year or <u>less</u>? How is that possible?"

For child actors, it's simple: children change every year. The entertainment business, like any other, runs in cycles. And in a business where timing is everything, your child might be the wrong age at the wrong time. This year, the demand may be for nine-year-old boys. Next year, the push may be for six-year-old girls. Even your child's agent can't explain it. So how do you survive? You hang in there, that's how! In two years, casting directors may be looking for eight-year-old boys and it just so happens you've got one!

For this reason and many more, it is important for you, your child and his agent to be happy with each other. A good children's agent is often hard to find, but when you secure one, you'll probably discover a person with a rewarding career who loves discovering new talent and helping these youngsters take their first steps toward stardom.

WHEN SHOULD YOU CHANGE AGENTS?
That's easy: when the agent is no longer sending your child out on calls. If your child's agent is getting him in to see casting directors, she is doing her job; it's often difficult to get a casting agent to see a newcomer. As we've this before . . . AGENTS DON'T BOOK JOBS . . . CASTING DIRECTORS DO. Landing a job is up to your child, not his agent.

Utilize caution when approached by other agents offering you the moon. Agent-hopping can be a disaster for those who do it. Agents have feelings, too, and none of them enjoys losing a client to the unethical strategies of a competitor. It happens time and again in this business, with little, if any, satisfaction to the actor's career.

Try to remember when you landed representation for your child—that magical day when someone saw what you see in your child, and because life is full of surprises, your child stood up and was counted. You could find that, in six months, your child is the star of the future. (Now is a good time as any to beware of the dangling carrots.) Let's say he starred in a high-visibility commercial and his face is seen by millions. Is it any wonder every agent will want to represent him? But, remember: your child and his agent are responsible for his recent success. His current agent discovered him and took a chance on him when no one else would; your child succeeded in displaying that certain something which launched his career. So what's wrong with the agent who originally saw his talent? The agent isn't shocked or surprised at your child's new found success. She had faith in him; she believed it would happen all along. She's the one who took him on, remember? She personally shielded and ad-

vised him. She showed him the ropes. So don't be misled by offers from those agents who cannot find and groom new talent; these agents usually operate by nabbing successful clients from other agencies. Keep in mind, it's not <u>who</u> butters your bread, but who gave you any <u>bread</u> to butter in the first place.

Actors who "agent hop" usually wind up disillusioned and dissatisfied; they spend time and energy changing agents, trying to replace what they already had in the first place. One of the most significant keys to success in this industry is endurance and one of the greatest necessities for a long and flourishing career is having someone who believes in your child besides <u>you</u>! And not just for the season or the year, but for the duration! There are times of feast and famine in this business and you and your child will need a solid relationship with your agent to weather both. When you've found that person, hold on to her and don't be sidetracked by others—the most important consideration for a successful career in the industry is endurance. If your agent is getting you out on the calls, and is demonstrating a sincere interest in you and your child's career, you're not necessarily going to find better elsewhere, no matter what the other guy tells you.

On the other hand, if you feel like asking the agent, "What have you done for us lately?" because you haven't heard from her in months, or because she wouldn't recognize your child if he ran her down with his two-wheeler, it's best to move on. You don't have the right representation for your child.

All right. You've met and interviewed an agent who is willing to represent your child. It feels too good to be true, doesn't it? Don't stop to pat your-self on the back: you've still got a long road ahead. You've only just begun.

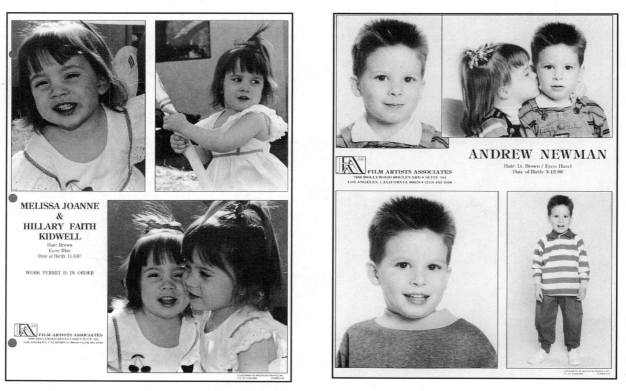

Sometimes you can get two for the price of one with siblings, especially when first starting out.

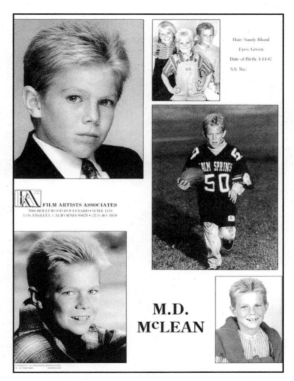

8

Professional Pictures

Your child must have <u>professional</u> pictures taken. (Yes, <u>professional</u>!)

The most important tool for any actor is his picture! You wouldn't ask your dentist to fix your teeth without the proper equipment, so, don't send your child out on his first interview without a good picture. This is what the casting directors use when selecting the actors they want to interview or audition.

Your agent probably could recommend several photographers, however, SAG suggests you choose the photographer on your own.

WHO PAYS FOR THE PICTURES?

Who else but you! They're pictures of <u>your</u> child that will be used by <u>your</u> child's agent to get <u>your</u> child out on calls, right? These pictures will bring <u>your</u> child work (hopefully) and the agent will get 10 percent of <u>your</u> child's pay, which is hardly enough for her to bear the cost of his photos.

Let's recap. This has been an exhilarating adventure so far, more fun than work. You like the idea of having a famous child actor in the family. You like day dreaming about seeing your child accept an Academy Award—the youngest Best Actor winner in history! You liked finding your child's agent. But now, you've stepped into another area altogether . . . you're expected to spend <u>money</u>. Nobody told you it was going to cost you money! The vision of your child's name in lights may start to fade at this point. It may effect your pocket book and he hasn't even worked yet! Everyone may think your child is cute, but, no one has made any promises that he ever will work! Do you drop out, or do you press on. You must go on, of course! You might have the next Elijah Wood (*The War* with Kevin Costner) or Ariana Richards (*Jurassic Park*). Who will expose this talent if you don't?

That's the spirit. Onward we go.

HOW MUCH SHOULD PROFESSIONAL PHOTOGRAPHS COST?

It varies, depending on whether you want a five-picture composite (five different pictures of him on one sheet) or just a head shot. This decision will be made by your child's agent.

Your child's knows how she wants to represent him; she has the job of selling his talent; she's the one with the experience; she'll make the decision about his photos. All you need do is pay for them.

You'd like to spend as little as possible; there's nothing wrong with shopping carefully. But cheap is cheap and if you're too frugal, you'll get what you pay for. Keep in mind, however, that photographers are sometimes willing to negotiate. If you're very nice and you're really good at begging for things, you can probably get him to lower his price a little. But, most photographers charge what they charge.

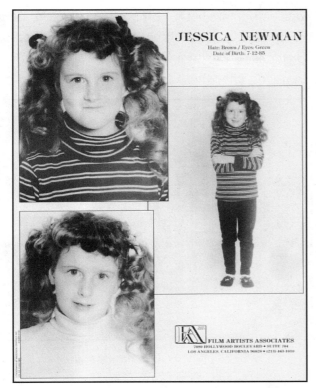

Here's what you get for little money (around $75).

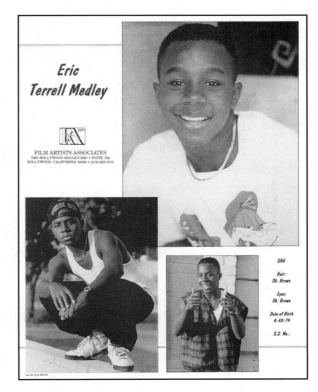

Here's what you get for a lot of money (around $250).

If you want the photographer to shoot three rolls of film with thirty-six exposures on each roll (you'll typically get four or five 8 x 10s out of the deal), the cost should be in the neighborhood of $225 to $300. However, market prices for photographs fluctuate with the economy as do real estate prices. And, much like the real estate market, prices for pictures may level off from year to year but they rarely go down! While the above estimate is not etched in stone, we would suggest not paying more than $300 for your child's pictures as you are just starting out. Depending on his age, it is possible all that you need to launch your child's career is a head shot, which can be done for $75 to $100. Your agent will advise you which way to go for your child.

"But I have a <u>friend</u> who is a photographer," you utter. Unless your friend is a professional photographer who has experience shooting children's composites, you are better off not using him. You'll have much more success if you let a professional photographer—one with experience working with children—do the job.

The result of an amateur photographer.
The twins are three years old.

The same set of twins shot by a professional, theatrical photographer.

It's a good idea to look at composites of other children before stepping into the studio with your child. You'll get better ideas from looking at other composites than from studying ads in magazines.

Your child—a newcomer to the business—needs a great picture more than the child who has already proven himself in the industry. Although it is possible to get away with a single head shot—one that will sell your child's face—a composite with different facial expressions is the most popular and the most successful.

True, a single head shot is cheaper, but a good composite catches the eye of casting agents quickly. Remember, casting agents look through hundreds of pictures daily, but they select only those with terrific

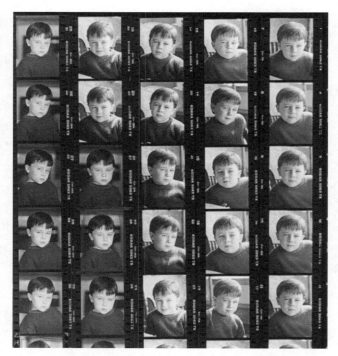

Sometimes a professional photographer will shoot an entire roll of film in order to get one good shot.

eye-catching looks (we're not talking about beauty . . . we're talking about sparkle). As we've said previously, your child's pictures are the most important "tools" of his trade.

So, contact several photographers and hire the best one you can afford.

THE PHOTO SHOOT
To get a good idea of how a photo shoot works, we'll describe a session for a full-five shot composite, which means five different outfits and expressions using three to six rolls of film.

More than likely, you'll bring your child to the photographer's studio or to an outdoor location the photographer suggests. (It has become more popular over the years to shoot children outdoors, where children are more relaxed, than under the hot lights of a photography studio.)

WARDROBE FOR THE PHOTO SHOOT

You'll bring the clothes your child will wear during his photo shoot, but the photographer will tell you the types of clothing to bring. Before the session, it's helpful to describe your child so the photographer will have a mental picture of him, such as his age, physical stature, plus extras, like his flaming red hair or his missing two front teeth. It's best, of course, if the photographer comes to your home, your child will be in comfortable surroundings and you'll have your child's full wardrobe at the photographer's disposal. Some photographers will come to your home, but don't be disappointed if yours says no. A natural outdoor background is very often a plus in composites.

Melissa Ann Martin
Hair: Brown
Eyes: Brown
D.O.B 11-16-85

FILM ARTISTS ASSOCIATES

A good head shot can be used for commercial and theatrical submissions by your agent.

HOW DO I CHOOSE THE RIGHT CLOTHES FOR THE SHOOT?
Selecting the wardrobe is not difficult if you follow a few simple guidelines.

★ The best are everyday clothes (the type your child wears to school or to play outside). Try a shirt with wide horizontal stripes and a pair of blue jeans—casting directors love this look.

★ They should be loose fitting; avoid that shirt or pair of pants you'd like him to get more wear out of.

★ Dress clothes (shirt, slacks, pull-over sweater) are okay, but are rarely used, unless your agent is seeking a more sophisticated look.

★ Holes in jeans or well-worn clothes sometimes add a different dimension.

★ Your child's old, tattered sweatshirt (the one you have been wanting to throw out) is a good choice: this type of clothing photographs well and your child will be thrilled to wear his favorite piece of clothing. (A child will be more

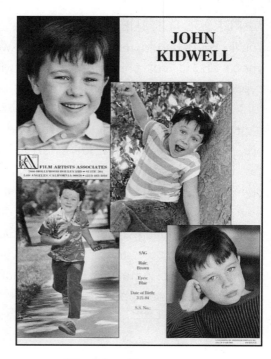

When shooting a composite, several sets of wardrobe should be worn.

relaxed and act more like himself when he's comfortable.)

★ Bring clothing that represents your child's special talent, such as his hockey or karate uniform, her ballet outfit, etc. If your child has a special talent, don't be afraid to advertise it. (For instance, when *Hook* was cast, the director was looking specifically for boys who had gymnastic training and could perform flips and somersaults, etc. A picture of your child executing a back flip is positive proof that he has this ability and, more than likely, would have resulted in an interview with the casting agents.)

★ Bring sporting equipment, such as a bike, roller blades or skateboard. (You can see now why you're ahead of the game if the session can take place at your home.)

Bring a dozen or so outfits for the photographer to choose from. Don't forget shoes and accessories, like hats, belts, jewelry, glasses, etc.

81

WHAT ARE THE WRONG KIND OF CLOTHES?

Clothes in white, red and black, and heavily-patterned shirts and sweaters are not good choices. Neither are fancy suits, tuxedos or party dresses. Also, don't bring any clothing with name brands or recognizable or readable writing or logos. Since the final pictures will be black and white, matching colors isn't important, as long as you're not putting stripes with plaids.

And, forget about

ERIC TERRELL MEDLEY
HAIR : DARK BROWN / EYES : DARK BROWN
D.O.B. : 4-30-79 / S.S.#

FILM ARTISTS ASSOCIATES
7080 HOLLYWOOD BOULEVARD • SUITE 704
HOLLYWOOD, CALIFORNIA 90028 • (213) 465-1010

turtlenecks. While they may look adorable to you, they do not frame the face nicely. (If you think about it, how many times have you seen them on children in commercials or motion pictures? Rarely, if ever!)

WHEN IS THE BEST TIME FOR THE SHOOT?

The best time for pictures is when the sun is shining. If your child's session is scheduled on a day that looks like rain, reschedule it. Select a time of day when your child is most animated and extroverted, for instance a week-end mid-morning. Conversely, if your child is exhausted when he comes home from school, don't schedule his photo shoot for 4:00 P.M. He'll be tired and cranky and everyone's time will be wasted, along with your money!

HOW ABOUT MAKEUP?
Again, remember, Mom and Dad, this is not a beauty pageant! That means no makeup for interviews and no makeup for photo

shoots. The photographer will be able to cover tiny scrapes or bruises, if need be, but he will not use makeup to cover freckles or change the contour of your child's nose or lengthen eyelashes.

Don't try to give your daughter the perfect model look; theatrical agents do not handle models. And, casting directors do not want children with any kind of affectations; children should be natural at all times. You'll probably hear people mention how far modeling has taken some kids. Pay no attention. Advertising people may want models who can strike a pose, but, film people prefer <u>real</u> kids.

WHO DECIDES WHICH PICTURES TO USE?
Once the proofs or contact sheets are ready, who selects the pictures? Your agent and you do. Keep in mind that your child's agent should have a bigger say, because she is the one with the experience in this area. She has likely seen thousands of pictures and knows what works and what doesn't.

After the shots are selected, the photographer will make enlargements (8 x 10s). Let your agent show you how to put them together into an interesting and pleasing fashion that best shows off your child.

Once you have received the enlargements, you will need to take them to a photography lab that will put the composite together and run off copies. Yes, you will need copies, lots of copies (300 is a good starting number, but ask your child's agent how many she'll need). The more you order, the cheaper the per-picture price will be. If your agent recommended a head shot (for theatrical calls) as well as a composite (for commercial calls), you will need multiple copies of each. As well as the agent

JEFFREY CATON

Michael Robert Chacon
Hair: Brown Eyes: Brown
D.O.B.: 7/3/92 SS#

using them, your child must have one for every audition, which he will leave with the casting agents at each call. There are times when the agents send out a photo and your child is not called in; these photos are not returned. Unfortunately for you, casting directors do not keep photos of children around for long periods of time because children change so rapidly.

In all likelihood, your child's agent will give you the photo lab her agency uses regularly; the lab will have the agency's logo on file and will be familiar with how the agency likes composites laid out.

WHAT INFORMATION GOES ON A HEAD SHOT OR COMPOSITE?

The composite or head shot should include the following information: your child's name; agency name (not the agent's name), its phone number and address; your child's date of birth; hair color; eye color; and if appropriate, the unions your child belongs to.

The photo lab probably will have a variety of layouts from which to choose, showing you the different positions of information and pictures. If your child requires only a head shot, the information will be printed at the bottom of the picture.

The cost of 300 copies of your child's head shot or composite will probably cost between $100 and $175, the first time it is made. After that, the cost should be slightly less because the lab will have your child's layout on file. When you need more copies, you need only call the lab and order more (via credit card), or you can re-order by mail (via check).

When it's time for new photographs altogether, you will need to start the process all over again.

After a discussion with your child's agent, you'll figure out when your child needs new photographs taken (it depends on how rapidly your child changes).

RESUMES

Your child will need a resume, even if he hasn't worked yet. Don't make up credits! Casting agents will know if the credits are fictitious and so will his agent. In the beginning, his resume should list his abilities, talents,

Good head shot.

A great commercial composite. Note the use of the head shot from the previous page in the composite layout.

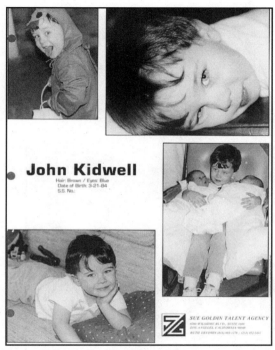

A non-professional composite. Note the difference between this and the one at left.

REBECCA
NEWMAN

FILM ARTISTS ASSOCIATES
7080 HOLLYWOOD BOULEVARD • SUITE 704
LOS ANGELES, CALIFORNIA 90028 • (213) 463-1010

Hair: Brown / Eyes: Brown
Date of Birth: 3-20-89
S.S. No.:

education, size information and training. After he starts working, some of the miscellaneous information will be replaced by his credits and his union status. (If he has worked one SAG job, his resume should indicate he is "SAG READY" or "SAG MUST" which will let casting know he must join the union on his next job.)

JOHN CHRISTOPHER KIDWELL
Film Artists Associates
(213) 555-6666 - Ruth Devorin

SAG

Hair: Brown
Eyes: Blue

SS#: 000-00-0000
DOB: 3/21/84

THEATRICALS:
"The Nutty Nut" - role of "36 inch Filbert"
    Nutty Nut Productions

MOWS:
"The President's Child" - starring role of Jason - CBS
"Shattered Dreams" - supporting role of "Mark" - CBS

TELEVISION APPEARANCES:
"Bodies of Evidence" (CBS) - guest star role of "Jimmy"
    (episode title - The Edge)
"Step By Step" (ABC) - guest star role of "Scotty"
    (episode title - Yo Yo's Wedding)
"Quantum Leap" (NBC) - guest star role of "Hank"
    (episode title - Heart of a Champion)

COMMERCIALS:
Numerous. List available upon request.

OTHER:
Children's books on tape with Robert Guillaume
Confetti Productions
Multiple Voice Over Characters

THEATRE:
John has performed in a variety of productions with his church
and his school.

SPECIAL TALENTS:
John is an excellent shot with a rifle, a good swimmer, rides a
bicycle, roller blades, skateboards and plays most sports.

Sample resume with lots of credits.

MELISSA JOANNE KIDWELL
(Melissa is an identical twin)
SS# 000-00-0000
SAG

Representation: FAA
Ruth Devorin
(213) 555-6666

Hair: Brown
Eyes: Hazel
DOB: 11/03/87
Dress Size: 6X

CREDITS:
"The Pretender" - (New series for NBC 1996 fall season)
    Supporting role - Twin #2

COMMERCIALS:
List available upon request.

TALENTS:
Studied tap, ballet and acrobatics since 1994 with Jean Reese.
Sings, dances, strong reader and excellent with memory work.

SPORTS:
Roller skates, rides a two wheel bike, jump ropes, excellent
baseball player, loves soccer and is very athletic.

MISCELLANEOUS:
Has performed in a variety of musical, variety and dance
programs with her dance school.

Sample resume with few credits.

– NOTES –

9

The Look

The most frequently question of asked an agent by a parent is: "Can you guarantee that my child will work?" We've already told you that there are no guarantees in this business. Agents are not casting directors or producers; they are not magicians, nor do they predict the future (at least none we've met). An agent, however, does guarantee to submit your child's picture and to give one heck of a pitch for any project that she feels is appropriate.

When casting, many topics are considered, including:

AGE

Casting agents are sometimes very specific about age requirements, especially if they need children under twelve months. This is one reason why your child's date of birth should appear on his composite. The age requirement usually broadens as children get older.

All children under six years qualify as "infants" and are limited to the amount of hours they can work in front of the camera. If school is in session, a child actor is required by law to receive three hours of schooling for every day he is filming. If

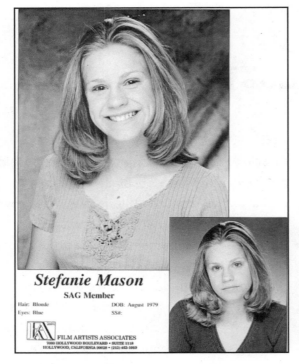

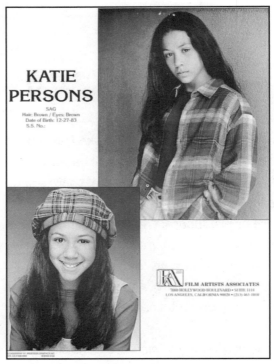

Two-photo composites are popular. One should be a great smile and the other should be a serious or character pose.

school is not in session, the child can work his full allotment of hours in front of the camera, as long as regulations (i.e., break periods and mealtimes) are met.

No minor may begin work earlier than 5:00 A.M. The workday must end no later than 10:00 P.M. on evenings preceding school days, 12:30 A.M. on mornings of non-school days. We're not saying that your child will be working from 5:00 A.M. to 12:30 A.M.; these are mandated starting and finishing times. Within these parameters, a child may work in front of the camera only for the number of hours regulated by his age. To monitor all of this, a teacher with appropriate credentials is provided on the set.

The number of hours a child is allowed to work grows as his age increases, until he becomes legal at eighteen years. If an actor over eighteen works longer than ten hours in a day, he is paid overtime. (This is one reason why an eighteen-year-old actor who looks younger than his age is considered a plus in the industry.) A child who is under the age of eighteen but is an emancipated minor (released from parental care) is also a plus. Emancipated children are considered adults, in most cases.

GENDER

Sometimes the call is only for boys or only for girls. For example, there's no need to see boys when casting a doll commercial. Sometimes, gender doesn't matter as much as a specific age group. Casting agents cast roles according to criteria submitted by the producer and/or director; the casting department is not responsible for creating the description of the character.

RACE

There may be a call for an ethnic child; sometimes the call is for "all" children.

TYPE

Another oft-asked question of an agent is, "Do you think my child has the right look?" No matter what ethnicity your child is, whether he is tall or short, thin or fat, blue-eyed or brown-eyed, the answer to this question is an emphatic "Yes!" And, we don't even have to see your child! Your child's attitude and personality should be your primary considerations in seeking a career for him, not his looks! Yes, there are countless adorable children in front of the camera, but that's because they are intelligent, have good attitudes, sparkling personalities and, most importantly, talent! (Contrary to popular opinion, looks alone do not get actors anywhere in this business.)

Go to the movies or watch television and you'll see for yourself what types of kids are working today . . . all kinds! Tall, short, thin, chubby, blonde or brunette, brown eyes or blue, casting agents are searching for unusual looks in children as well as girl- and boy-next-door-types. The demand for children of all types is never ending in this business. The point is, children are not judged by looks alone. In fact, they are most often judged by personality and the ability to learn dialogue. So, it doesn't matter whether or not your child is considered "beautiful." Sparkle is sparkle! And when you've got it, you've got it!

KATRINA CONTRERAS

Raushan Hammond
SAG / AFTRA

A relaxed, natural smile will capture the eye of the casting director in a hurry.

Sometimes it only takes two pictures to show it all.

GIMMICK

A gimmick is a quality or physical attribute that stands out as memorable, for instance, a deep or unusual voice (like the original Froggy in *The Little Rascals* series). A speech impediment falls in this category, as do exaggerated ears or huge dimples. However, after the age of six, such gimmicks can actually start to turn against the child actor. (Lisping at age two is cute; lisping at age twelve represents a problem with speech development.)

ATTITUDE

The most important quality a child actor can have is a good attitude, a willingness to do the job. (This applies to the parents, as well.) In fact, keeping the child actor's attitude in check is one of the most difficult challenges for the new stage parent. Because many of you, at the beginning are working parents, it is especially difficult to chauffeur your child to interviews and auditions. But, if you want your child's attitude to remain positive, you should be sure to do the chauffeuring. It's tempting to hire someone to do all the driving, so you won't have to quit your job or worse, risk getting fired. However, you and your child are in this <u>together</u> and you should take him on calls! Occasionally, schedules conflict (especially if you have more than one child in the industry); if this is the case, a close relative or friend is an acceptable substitute, but for the most part, the parent should accompany his own child. If you can't make a call with your child, don't be a pest by asking him about the interview. Understand the responsibility and accept it.

This a time of learning, especially in the beginning, and you have as much to learn, if not more,

than your child. It's an easy business if <u>you</u> don't do any work and your child won't be successful with this kind of attitude. There is no such thing as halfway in this business . . . your commitment must be solid. If you're not 100% ready and willing, you might as well abandon ship, because you will sink fast.

ODDS
How many kids work in the business? The statistics vary but our guess is that 10 percent to 20 percent of all child actors work on a regular basis. But, we're not talking about making millions of dollars, we're talking about working.

They are not necessarily the same children from year to year and this industry is one in which there is always room for one more. Our guess of 10 percent to 20 percent of children who book jobs does not include the children who do not yet have their union cards or have worked only one job. Stop and think for a minute: Doesn't it seem to you that you're seeing a new young face on TV every time you turn it on? Well, you are. (Most of the actors whose photographs appear in this book have or have had successful careers.) There are many children who work one time and never again. Why? Sometimes they get tired; they may not like the work and quit before their big break; the parents may have difficulty managing their child's career. And, there are those who opt to trade in the world of fame and fortune for a more normal life style that includes regular school, college, a social life, family, friends, all the elements that took a beating while they were working.

Sometimes your child will find the plus that got him launched in the business will turn against him

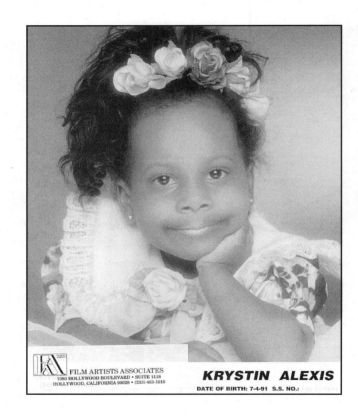

FILM ARTISTS ASSOCIATES
7080 HOLLYWOOD BOULEVARD • SUITE 1118
HOLLYWOOD, CALIFORNIA 90028 • (213) 463-1010

KRYSTIN ALEXIS

DATE OF BIRTH: 7-4-91 S.S. NO.:

JOHN KIDWELL
Hair: Brown / Eyes: Blue
Date of Birth: 3-21-84 / S.S. No.:

FA FILM ARTISTS ASSOCIATES
7080 HOLLYWOOD BOULEVARD • SUITE 1118
LOS ANGELES, CALIFORNIA 90028 • (213) 463-1010

as he ages. For instance, we have mentioned that a child who is small for his age is a positive in this business. (See the section on "Age," earlier in this chapter.) An older child can work longer hours in front of the camera; he also has an easier time learning lines and taking direction; he can jump higher, run faster, smile longer; he throws fewer tantrums and doesn't need naps! But sooner or later, things that had been attributes may start working against the child actor. For example, your fourteen-year-old may still look eleven, but maybe his voice is beginning to change. Or maybe he'll suddenly experience a major growth spurt.

TALENT

In the early days of the industry, a child actor was trained in voice, dance, drama, sports, acrobatics, ad infinitum. So competition was fierce! Today? It's not vastly different. If you're serious about your child's career, you should train him in every area where he has ability. However, at the very least, he should study acting. All talent must be trained and guided and every time your child works, he's getting better. Even natural-born performers continue to fine tune their craft; It's this determination to better their abilities that makes them excel.

There are many acting workshops and teachers for actors in the business. If you're earnest about having your child proceed in the industry, find a way to enroll him in acting school. Consider after-school programs, there are numerous theater workshops. Performing on stage is a most rewarding experience for an actor, because it's immediate self-gratification. The sound of applause can be matched by nothing to an actor.

For other kinds of lessons, e.g., in dance, athletics, gymnastics, karate, try your local department of parks and recreation, or private schools with professional training. Ask your agent, who should be a good resource of activities and lessons for children. They will be able to recommend something suitable for your child's age and your pocketbook.

When the casting company was casting The Lost Boys in *Hook*, it was seeking boys in a particular age range who had acrobatic and gymnastic experience. Whether the boy had two lines or fifty, he was a good athlete. Your child might be a gifted actor but he would not have gone on this call unless he had acrobatic or gymnastic abilities.

INDEPENDENCE
How independent is your child if left to his own devices? Do you speak for him or does he speak for

himself? Your child's ability to handle himself is as important as his ability to turn on the sparkle. If he's in a wardrobe fitting and the clothes are too tight, he needs to feel confident enough to tell the tailor. He should be brave enough to speak up for himself. You shouldn't have to prompt him. Nor should you put so much pressure on him about being polite and well-behaved that he clams up around crew members.

TEETH

Once your child starts to lose his teeth, he'll most likely need a flipper. Are we talking about the hit television series from the '70s? No. A flipper is a partial dental plate or, false teeth, which is removable (like a retainer) and is only worn while the child is in front of the camera. The flipper fills any gaps the child may have when he begins losing baby teeth.

Why in the world is this a concern? Most people who cast children believe that kids look better with front teeth. A flipper is strictly for cosmetic purposes, because growing children should not attach permanent bridgework in their mouths. However, you should know that flippers are expensive. And, because flippers are considered a <u>cosmetic</u> device, dental plans usually don't cover them. On an upbeat note, most kids only need flippers for a year or two, or until their permanent teeth grow in.

Straight teeth are as important for the child actor as they are for adult actors. Your child's teeth don't have to be perfect, but see for yourself how many child actors with crooked teeth are working . . . not many. Braces are an easy (albeit, expensive) remedy and straightening your child's teeth while he's working isn't a problem. Visible braces, however, can be problematic—especially if he hasn't yet worked. They are a deterrent for the child who is interested in commercial work because advertising people usually don't use kids with visible braces to advertise products. Visible braces limit children to roles in which the child is of feasible, braces-wearing age.

A better option is braces that bring your child's teeth into alignment while remaining invisible to the naked eye. Invisible braces aren't truly invisible; they are braces which are cemented to the back of the teeth as opposed to the front. They are more expensive than standard braces and they do the job in about the same time. However, they are cumbersome and sometimes create speech impediments.

Some consider the best option to be an appliance called a "crozat", which looks and functions like a retainer (and can be easily removed when the child is working), but works like braces. Crozats are about twice as expensive as braces and take about two and a half times longer to do the job. However, if your child is going out on a lot of calls, or if he starts booking many parts, you may have no other choice. Crozats will have a positive effect on his career, as well.

HAIR

There are wonderfully creative hair styles these days, but not all of them are suitable for the child actor. No matter how talented your child may be, he will not appear on a period show like *Dr. Quinn, Medicine Woman* if his hair is cut in a hip, '90s style. A casting agent may be reluctant to ask your child if he'll can cut his hair, especially if it's only for a couple lines or a commercial. The only way to avoid this is to keep his hair in a style that looks good on him, but that can be styled easily into a different 'do. Long hair can be cut and shaped; short hair grows back; unusual styles work only for contemporary jobs. Mohawks hardly ever work for any kind of job.

For girls, hair that is long enough to put in a ponytail or pigtails works best (below the shoulder). Short hair on girls works only for the tomboy look. Your child's hair style should look good on her and be versatile. Think natural; perms and Shirley Temple curls are a thing of the past. It's a definite plus if your child's hair is naturally curly; on the other hand, if you've told casting agents that her beautiful curls are natural and they're not, you'll watch in horror as her curls fall flat at the end of a long day in front of the camera.

NEVER cut your child's hair in-between auditions for the same project! We know of several instances when a child has lost a booking because his parent wanted to improve his look by restyling his hair. If you are in doubt as to the appropriate hair length for your child or when it should be cut, ask your agent; these are the kinds of decisions that should be left to her.

TRAINING

We don't mean the kind of training your child receives in acting class. This training is the learning process your child undergoe's by participating in the working process. A professional booking teaches your child a variety of things, among them, discipline. In addition, your child will learn how to hold a script for a reading when he hasn't memorized the lines; he'll learn not to cover his face with the script page; he'll learn how to project his voice without it sounding forced. You see, it's that same catch-22: your child learns how to perform a good audition only by auditioning; he learns how to work in front of the camera only when he is actually in front of the camera.

It is critical for actors to learn how to communicate body language and facial expressions, and to execute simple blocking; while these aspects can be learned in the classroom, performing them comfortably in front of the camera is a different story. Using facial expressions and body language when we're engaged in casual conversation is easy. That feeling of comfort must be "on call" and reproduced at every audition. Again, actual work experience is the best training of all. The more often your child goes out on calls, the more comfortable he will be with his body movements.

READING
The ability to read is an important for all actors.

The earlier your child can read, the better he will fare in this business, because he may not always have enough time to memorize lines. If your child is reading age, start teaching him. There are plenty of books and phonics courses on tapes. Please, parents, don't try to teach your two-year-old something he isn't ready to learn.

If your child is too young to read to himself, you should read to him. He will learn to recognize numbers, letters and words. Believe it or not, it will help him when he needs to memorize lines. And, you'll never feel closer to your child than when you read to him.

ACTORS WITH DISABILITIES
If your child is disabled and would like to try acting, there's no need to discourage him because this industry makes room for everybody! SAG has a spe-

cial form for actors with physical disabilities; a sample is included for your review. Call the SAG office in your area to receive one. This is the movie industry and everybody is welcome.

BEING DISCOVERED—IT COULD HAPPEN TO YOU

Can you be discovered in a Hollywood drugstore, eating a hamburger at the counter? It's rumored that Lana Turner was discovered this way. After the rumor hit, young hopefuls migrated to Hollywood to be discovered, like Lana, but with little success. Curious, isn't it?

It's different today. The industry is open to any actor, no matter where he lives. Coast-to-coast talent searches are organized frequently, whenever producers or directors are looking for a new, young actor to star in an upcoming movie. Now and then, a new talent will be discovered, like Mason Gamble (*Dennis The Menace*,

Sample SAG Disability Form.

Warner Bros., 1993) or Michael Conner Humphreys (*Forrest Gump*, Paramount, 1994) who played Forrest Gump as a young boy.

Sometimes, talent searches will make a newcomer a star; other times, they are nothing more than publicity stunts. (Hundreds of kids usually show up at open calls and all of them will go to the movie to see who won the part, thus benefiting the movie's box office gross.) Whether your child stands a chance or not, open calls are worth your time. Chalk it up to experience.

Leann Heng

– NOTES –

– NOTES –

10

Working Outside
Of The United States

If your child has booked a job outside of the United States, he will need a passport and a work visa, along with his work permit and social security number. Obtaining these documents is your responsibility, although assistance is provided by the movie's production staff. For example, the production office will give you the name and phone number of the doctor who will examine your child and administer the correct vaccines.

Movies are filmed all over the world and especially in countries such as Canada, England, Ireland, Australia and Mexico. Most often, the reason is economic, but the director may need an authentic location, or the producer may be concerned with union issues. In any case, it's a good idea to be prepared: both parents and all children in the family should have current passports. (The producer may surprise you and send the whole family!)

At any rate, a passport is one form of identification acceptable for the I-9 form.

Booking a job outside the United States is not likely to happen early in a child's acting career, but the possibility exists. (Your child could be discovered in one of those famous nationwide talent searches!)

But, don't worry! Since rules vary between countries, the producer will assist you with the details. If you have your child's passport, work permit and social security number, you're well ahead of the game. Remember, SAG doesn't have jurisdiction in other countries.

– NOTES –

– NOTES –

11

Responsibilities Of The Stage Mother

We could fill the Smithsonian with stories about stage mothers and stage fathers . . . what a cast of characters.

We're giving the stage mothers their chapter first because there are more of you out there than there are stage fathers. However, stage fathers, you'll enjoy reading this chapter as much, if not more than, the chapter we've dedicated to you.

Stage mothers can be celestial or monstrous (these are the women about whom the term "stage mother" has grown to mean a mother of great unpleasantness who is shepherding her child's acting career).

For new stage moms, it's hard to comprehend how much work goes into managing their child's acting career. Managing a family, particularly in this day and age, is difficult enough; adding a show business career for your child can make life even harder. There is much to learn as you go along your road to fame and fortune, because it's what you _don't_

<u>know</u> that can hurt you. Trust us, Mom, <u>your</u> attitude is everything! You don't need to be overpowering, demanding, pushy, whiny, complaining and generally disgruntled; these classic stage mothers are nightmares on the set and they don't even know it! However, everyone else knows it.

Luckily, this type of stage mother is no longer the norm; well-adjusted child actors in the industry far outnumber the tragic child actors you read about in the tabloids. (The well-adjusted, one-time child actors are off somewhere enjoying their lives as adults.) Most of these well-balanced young performers have affectionate and responsible parents to thank for their success and for their sound bodies and minds. They were raised by parents who listened, watched and guided their children carefully and most importantly, accepted their responsibilities as parents. You will meet other stage moms whom you will find to be good, nurturing and dedicated parents. Let them serve as an inspiration to you. So, as you help your child's career, please . . . don't transform into a reptilian woman who will stop at nothing to prove the greatness of her offspring. If you fit any part of this negative characterization, do something about it posthaste, for if you don't, the consequences could be catastrophic for you and your child.

Every once in a while, you'll run into a demonic stage mother whose child is successful. How is this conceivable? These moms may have very talented children; or, they may keep their true personalities hidden until their child is well-established. If you can't keep your perspective in check, you'll soon find that, no matter how talented your child is, you, the stage mother, will only be remembered as an experience not worth repeating.

JOBS THAT MOM ISN'T RESPONSIBLE FOR

The job of mom, although complex and broad, does not include the following:

Director . . . No, you won't be asked to direct; the producer already has hired the director of his choice for the project.

Producer . . . No, you may not do this job, either.. The producer got the project off the ground; he's the one who hired the director and your child. He won't be replaced by a stage mother.

Writer . . . No, there's no need to bring writing samples to the set with you. The script already has been written and if changes are necessary, they'll be made by the writer.

Set Designer, Makeup or Wardrobe . . . No openings here, either. And, don't rush to give makeup, hair or wardrobe people your tips. (Be especially careful about stepping on their toes; they carry scissors with them at all times!)

Once you've been around a set often enough, you'd be shocked at how uncontrollable the desire is to poke your nose where it doesn't belong. It can begin as simply as this: One day, you overhear the director talking to Wardrobe about what color pajamas your child should wear in for the next scene. In the very next instant, you're suggesting his favorite color because he loves it and it looks so good on him . . . .

If he's nice, the director will most likely move his conversation out of your earshot without replying to your comment! You'll be left standing there alone, feeling like an idiot. While producers, directors and crew members are regular people, when they're working, they control the magic; they hold the power. So, leave decisions (no matter how trivial they seem) up to them. However, there may be times when your opinion is solicited; by all means, offer it in a tactful, kind, supportive and honest way.

On the whole, we have found today's stage moms to be supportive, protective and cooperative parents who demonstrate a true sense of concern for their children. If you remember to keep the well-being of your child as your first priority, you will be doing your job. While caring for your child, you must exhibit discipline and you must control your child's behavior at all times.

Once your child has broken into the business and is working regularly, the two of you will be spending more time together than ever before. This will be some of the most valuable time you'll ever spend with him, so use it judiciously; engage in positive, supportive conversations; talk about topics that will keep your child's attention or about subjects that interest him; sing or play games; run the lines he has to know for the job or audition. Don't pressure him or tell him how important the job/audition is. The last thing he needs is an extra helping of urgency from mom! Your child should be confident and relaxed; he should not feel the pressure of performance until he walks through the door.

Always remember, Mom, he is your child and you love him, whether he becomes a successful actor or never books a job. You are both on this adventure because it is something fun to do together. If it stops being fun, why continue?

– NOTES –

117

– NOTES –

12

Responsibilities Of The Stage Father

Yes, there are indeed stage fathers, too! You won't see many as most kids go to calls with their mothers. We hope you read the previous chapter, because almost every tip we gave to the moms pertains to dads as well. Dads, just like the moms, your main objective is to give your child enough room to sparkle! So . . . lighten up! (Easier said than done, isn't it?)

Like stage mothers, stage fathers come from all walks of life. However, unlike the moms, there are a number of dads who were once in the industry themselves and who promote it to their children as a matter of family tradition. After all, the apple doesn't fall far from the tree.

For these dads, most of the following guidelines are extraneous because you are already familiar with the business. For the rest of you, we're offering you guidance on how to handle this new enterprise.

HOW DO YOU COPE?

If your child already has been on a number of auditions, let <u>him</u> tell you how it's done; he will know what to do—kids love to show their parents they know something. Your job, Dad, is getting him to the designated place on time and to make sure he feels confident when he arrives.

On the whole, dads are more easily discouraged than moms when it comes to the time it takes to launch a child in show business; dads want it to happen fast! If his child goes on four or five interviews and doesn't book a job, Dad might want to throw in the towel. Dads also seem to take it more personally when someone else books a job. Dads, get a grip! It's not rejection, it's <u>selection</u>! Also known as <u>casting</u>! The producer and director have a very specific look or type in mind; it rarely changes. That is, unless your child walks in the room and blows their minds with so much charm and ability that the casting people forget what they were looking for in the first place. If your child meets the match, it's great! If he doesn't, IT'S NOT HIS FAULT!

Don't forget, Dad, that if a child actor is needed, most likely, a set of adult actors are needed to play his parents. Your child must be matched up to these actors, making the casting process more complex.

The mystery of the unknown—like availability—is the type of show business element that makes stage dads go nuts! Control yourself, Dad. Remember, this business requires endless patience. Hopefully, there will come a time (if you persist long enough) when your child will start booking jobs. Once your child has finished his audition, move on. If the part is his, you'll hear about it!

At the beginning of this venture, your child may

wonder how he should react to the disappointments of not being called back or booking a job. You should always remember to offer positive reinforcement, whether he books the job or not. Here are two suggestions to let him know he's doing great: "Oh, boy. You were close that time," or "Your time is coming, I can just feel it." The best way to approach a career in this business is by being calm, joyful and hopeful. Your child will benefit from this experience, whether he works a lot or not at all. Certainly, he will gain more self-composure and self-assuredness; in fact, his successes and failures can be measured by the amount of joy he derives from his efforts.

So, Dad, don't intimidate your child! Keep telling yourself that you're there to help your child do a good job while having fun, too.

Resist the temptation to demand recognition for your child's career. He is responsible for his success because he's the one with the talent!

– NOTES –

13

The First Call

PRIOR TO THE AUDITION

Before your child goes out on a real honest-to-goodness audition, his agent has been sending his pictures to casting people based on descriptions for roles they receive everyday. These daily "breakdowns" specify the myriad of projects ready for production and the roles available in each one. They are strictly confidential; you can work a lifetime in this industry and never see one. However, we're giving you a peek at a breakdown so you'll be ahead of the game. The name of the casting company, the project and the characters have been changed to protect the innocent . . . (namely, us!)

When breakdowns are released, the agent contemplates which of her clients fits the description of a role being cast. (There are exceptions to this rule. For example, Raushan Hammond, pg. 95, in *Hook*, could hardly be considered for a role requiring acrobatics—but, oh, could he act.) Your agent will then choose clients that best fit the descriptions on the breakdowns and submit the actors' picture or place a phone call and then submit the picture.

The agent should inform casting of her client's

```
**************************************************
[ NAME OF BREAKDOWN SERVICE]         - BREAKDOWN #16
THIS IS CONFIDENTIAL, COPYRIGHTED INFORMATION — DO NOT COPY!!!

(2:45 P.M.)
*Addendum to 4/15 #34
[ NAME OF PRODUCT]        CASTING: [ CASTING COMPANY]
NATIONAL NETWORK & SPOT  SHOOTS: [ DATE]
                         INTERVIEWS: [ DATE]
                         CONFLICTS:  [ NAMES OF PRODUCTS
                                      ACTORS CAN' T HAVE
                                      RUNNING]


CALL IMMEDIATELY WITH NAMES TO:  [ CASTING COMPANY
                                   AND PHONE NUMBER]


Will give audition times when you call.

*DESPERATELY SEEKING—

ADDITIONAL AFRICAN-AMERICAN BABIES: 10-18 months, NO OLDER, 18
to 24 lbs.; must have perfect unblemished skin; NO moles. NO
scars. Skin tone/coloring should be medium chocolate—neither
dark, nor light—MEDIUM ONLY. Very friendly and open and not
afraid of strangers—actress mom. Will audition naked to show
off all that perfect skin . . .


COPYRIGHT (c) [ DATE AND NAME OF BREAKDOWN SERVICE] —-
ALL RIGHTS RESERVED (C)
**************************************************
```

Sample breakdown (commercial spot).

```
**************************************************
[ NAME OF BREAKDOWN SERVICE] [ PHONE NUMBERS] [ WARNING]
COPYRIGHT INFORMATION
[ NAME OF PRODUCTION COMPANY]
[ NAME OF THE PROJECT]
[ TYPE OF PROJECT: FEATURE FILM, MOW, ETC.]

Producer: [ Name]
Director: [ Name]
Writers: [ Name(s)]
Casting Directors: [ Name(s)]
Casting Associate: [ Name]
Start Date:
Location:

WRITTEN SUBMISSIONS ONLY TO:       [ NAME AND ADDRESS OF
                                     CASTING AGENCY]
```

A previous breakdown has been released for this project. PLEASE NOTE THE NEW FAX NUMBER ABOVE.

Please note that the following characters in this film are between 12 and 15 years old. If you have clients in this age range WHO HAVE NOT ALREADY BEEN SUBMITTED, please submit them immediately. SCRIPTS ARE AVAILABLE TO BE PICKED UP. This is a contemporary film.

MIKE: A wide eyed 12-year-old with a talent for baseball. Mike is outgoing, extremely thin and good natured. Other kids are constantly teasing him about his weight. What they don't realize is Mike is dying of AIDS . . . LEAD (12-14)

DAVID: A rough and tumble, street-wise 12-year-old. He is the star of the little league baseball team. He meets Mike when Mike moves in next door. They immediately become friends. David decides to help Mike get on the baseball team . . . LEAD (12-14)

CAROL: Mike's sister. She is tall and thin. Her face is worn from the strain caring for her sick brother has brought. She is not willing to let him join with others for fear someone will discover Mike's illness and he will be an outcast . . . SUPPORTING (13-15)
```
**************************************************
```

Sample breakdown (theatrical project).

extra talents. For example, she'll promote the fact that her client is, let's say he's four years old, and he plays the piano and does the splits. (Every little "extra" talent that your child owns is a plus, even if it's not required for the job.) Remember, however, there are countless agents all over town submitting pictures of their clients who are also four, play the piano and can do the splits, so that extra talent is not necessarily a shoo-in for your child.

In the beginning, your child will likely go out on more commercial calls than theatrical because, as a novice performer, he has a better chance of booking a one-day job than the lead in a movie with a twelve-week shooting schedule. Also, advertising people are always looking for new faces to promote their products! Usually producers and directors of movies prefer accomplished actors because the pressures of filming a motion picture are great. Un-til your child acquires experience (i.e., a page of credits), auditions for movie roles are something he should strive for. Right now he should work on booking smaller jobs; the big jobs will follow.

As a side note to the auditioning process, no, the agent does not pester the casting people as to how her clients did on any particular audition. You must learn patience. If anyone would know how they did, it should be you. After all, you were there. The agent usually likes to hear how the child fares from the parent. It's important for you to be honest. If the child had a bad call, let the agent know the reason. Honesty is the best policy. If there is trouble in paradise, the agent will hear about it.

GETTING THE AUDITION

After the casting people have reviewed the pictures, they will call the agents and tell them who they want to schedule for interviews. Your agent, in turn, will call you with the following information:

The name and address of the casting director and/or casting company; the name of the project your child will be auditioning for; where to pick up the sides (lines); the date and time of the call; what to wear; when the job shoots. Plus, she'll tell you what is expected of your child and any other pertinent information.

Your agent may not know the following:

1.) Directions to the call (locate the address with your own map, which you'll need and use).

2.) How much it pays. Most likely, it will be scale plus 10 percent—or better. It will be union (SAG or AFTRA).

3.) Where to park. (You must figure this one out on your own. Allow plenty of time.)

ARE YOU PREPARED?

If you have a long drive to the audition, let your child nap in the car. However, if he usually does not wake happily from a nap, allow yourself extra time so he'll be able to wake up fully before he must speak to the casting agents.

Take a copy of your child's picture; the casting people already have seen it but you will need another to leave at the audition. You don't need the work permit; that is necessary only when your child is working. You may get a call in the morning scheduling an audition for that afternoon but you will never be asked to take your child out of school for it; it's against the law. You may take your child out of school to work, however, as there is a social worker/studio teacher assigned to him to give the three hours of required schooling. Cancel any extra curricular activities (lessons, games, etc.) if they interfere with the audition time; agents cannot set times that are "convenient" for you or your child. You have one chance at an audition . . . take it! If you start missing calls for any reason other than illness, your agent may drop you without warning.

WHAT TO DO WHEN YOU ARRIVE
AT THE AUDITION

When you arrive at the call, find the sign-in sheet and sign in your child so the casting agents know that he has arrived.

The sign-in sheet should be somewhere in plain view, usually on a table outside the casting office door where your child will audition. More than likely, there will be other parents signing in their children, so follow them. Check the top of the sheet; it lists the job. (You don't want to sign in for a cereal commercial on a car commercial sign-in sheet. Also,

sign-in sheets are used by the guild to verify union time.) You also must fill in size sheets with information about your child's sizes, etc. Size sheets are used by the wardrobe information, so make sure they are accurate.

This is a typical size sheet. You will fill out one of these every time your child auditions. Make sure all the information is current.

To ensure accuracy, measure and weigh your child regularly, keeping track of his current height, weight and wardrobe sizes. At most auditions, a Polaroid photograph of your child will be taken and attached to his size sheet. (Yes, this occurs, even though you've brought a picture with you.)

If there are sides (lines or dialogue) to be learned, these will be on the table next to the sign-in sheet (if you were not able to pick them up prior to the call). It's your responsibility to rehearse this material with your child, preparing him for his audition. If there are no lines, you might find a "storyboard" posted on the wall illustrating the action to be filmed. Your child might be asked to do some improvisation related to the storyboard. Have him practice expressions or as seen in the storyboard. For instance, if the board shows a boy tiptoeing past his sleeping father, have your child practice the same movements. When you're rehearsing with him, remember to be positive. If he's not doing the action the way you think he should, praise him anyway, but suggest that he do it a different way and add more movements. For casting people, _more_ is always _better_. (If your child takes direction well and is a good listener, the casting agents can always get him to do _less_ but it's much more difficult to get a child to do _more_!) Of course, more is better.

```
┌──────────────────────────────────────────┐
│ Please fill out this card completely      │
│ Name: _____  Date: _____ │
│ Address: _____  Agent: _____ │
│ Phone: _____  Phone: _____ │
│ Service: _____  SAG Member Yes __ No __│
│ Height: _____  Weight _____ │
│ Under 18, Date of Birth _____ │
│ Suit/Dress: _____  S.S.# _____ │
│ Shirt/Bust: _____  Waist: _____ │
│ Hair Color: _____               │
│ Hips: _____  Inseam: _____  Age Range: __│
│ Hat: _____  Glove: _____  Seen for: ___│
│ Shoe: _____  Special Skills: _____ │
│ _____ │
└──────────────────────────────────────────┘
```

Sample size sheet

When his audition time arrives, it's time for him to focus! That means you, too, Mom! Don't prattle on with the other moms. Focus! Rehearse lines or practice action.

Casting directors usually call actors in the order they arrive (hence the importance of the sign-in sheet.) As each audition is completed, another name is checked off. After a few auditions, you can judge how long each audition is taking then assess how much time you and your child have to prepare. Younger children are usually asked to memorize the lines; older children are allowed to "cold read" if they can keep their eyes on the person they're reading while glancing at the page only occasionally.

No matter how many auditions your child has been on, remind him that he is going to talk to people without you present. This is especially important with younger children. It's a good idea to have several conversations on this topic especially prior to your child's first auditions. Remind him of his interview with his agent which will give him a feeling of familiarity.

The most important business at hand is for your child to be lucid about what is expected of him in the audition. Make sure he knows the lines and movements. When his name is called, don't fuss over him or bark instructions at him; hand him his picture, his size sheet, his script and let him go. (Eventually, he will gather these things himself.) No prolonged good-byes, hugs or kisses. A word or look of encouragement is all he needs.

Inside the casting room, your child will be asked to "slate"—give the casting people his name, age and sometimes, the name of his agency. A brief conversation with the casting director may ensue. Then he will be asked to read his lines. If his reading goes well, he may be asked to read (or say) his lines again. (Nearly all auditions are videotaped now.) When the audition is over, he will be excused. Sign him out on the "sign-in sheet," which is collected by the Guild to ensure that actors are not held longer than the union allows.

SAG has a time limit on how long any actor can be held on a call. For example, on a *commercial* call, if your child is left waiting for more than an hour past his scheduled time, the company must compensate SAG $50 which is then paid to your child.

THE IMPORTANCE OF ACTING LESSONS

We'd like to reemphasize the importance of acting lessons, because this is the only place where children can practice their craft in an en-

Sample Sign-In Sheet

vironment where they can learn from their mistakes.

If your child's only practice area is at auditions, he'll lose ground. Remember, you are not in the room during the audition so you don't know the difficulties your child encounters, nor would you be objective about them. A good acting coach or theater group easily identifies acting problems and will offer constructive criticism in a positive manner. Keep in mind that your child aspires to be a <u>professional</u> actor; let him learn his craft from a professional.

Polaroids are taken and attached to your child's size sheet before being seen by casting.

WHAT NOT TO DO DURING AN AUDITION

Keep in mind that natural, "real" children are considered a plus; so don't fuss with your child in the casting area. It will make for a stressful situation and can transform your happy, prepared little actor into a sassy, uncooperative, little monster. Furthermore, casting directors have been known to call the agents of children with fussing moms or dads and complain because one child's stressed-out behavior can disrupt the entire waiting room.

You will *go* on many calls with other auditioning actors and the crowded room can become boisterous. Make sure your child does not demolish the room where you are waiting. The manner in which a parent disciplines his offspring is usually well-noted by the casting people. They'll assume that if your child is wild in the waiting room, he'll likely be uncontrollable in front of the camera. You may think this business is filled with little monsters, but it isn't!

It's fine for your child to talk with other children, but he should never be allowed to run, push, shove, yell or otherwise disturb the others. Most likely, the casting office is working on several projects at once; one ill-behaved child will disturb every actor who is preparing for his audition.

A WORD TO THE WISE
On the whole, show business is overflowing with skilled, talented, luminous and acquiescent child actors. (Now and then, a little terror or two may enjoy some success.) But you'll find that discipline is a key element to your child's survival rate in this industry and is critical to his success. An unmanageable child is seldom hired, since it is doubtful that he is adequately grounded to meet the challenges required of a child actor.

It should be noted that only children who are doing well in school are able to work. For instance, only a child with satisfactory grades (i.e., "C" average or above in grades; "satisfactory" or above in performance) will be issued a work permit in the State of California. However, each state has its regulations, so check your state's Department of Social Services or your child's agent.

Most kids will be noncommittal when asked by their parents how the audition went. Although frustrating for parents, this is the healthiest attitude a child can have. Don't get your feathers ruffled; it was just an audition. He did his best. Most younger children can't tell the difference between the audition and the actual job. He may feel he's done three or four jobs just because he was videotaped every time! Why spoil it for him? If he feels good about it, you should feel good about it, too!

– NOTES –

14

The Callback

The first real feeling of excitement over your child actor comes with the callback. You'll feel like part of the "in crowd" as soon as you hang up the phone.

Hopefully, your child's agent will be sending him on lots of calls, so neither your nor your child will be sitting around waiting for the phone to ring. But one day it will (sometimes as long as three weeks after his audition) and you'll learn that your child got a callback. Boy, what a feeling!

First, let your child know that he's a champion; get excited and celebrate the moment. (If you wait until he books the job to congratulate him, you may be waiting a very long time!) But remember: he still hasn't been hired yet.

DEALING WITH THE PRESSURE

Now the pressure's on! You already know he was well-liked because he got a callback. But what made them like him? What did he do that was so special? Was it the way he delivered his lines? Was it his smile? The most trying part of the callback process is figuring out what your child in his audition that caught someone's attention—and then trying to get him to do it again!

The director is often present at callbacks; after all, as he's the one who makes the final casting decisions. Do you remember that all auditions are now videotaped? They're videotaped for the director. Once he views all the audition tapes, he narrows the competition. Those still in the running are brought back to read for him. You can try to get your child to reconstruct the audition, but it will probably be a futile exercise.

WHAT TO DO AT THE CALLBACK
Unless told otherwise by your agent, have your child wear the same clothes he wore to the first audition. Don't try for "a better look." Caution your child to listen to what is said to him and to respond when spoken to. (These are important points on any call.) A shake of the head as a response to a question won't leave a good impression. A spoken response—not merely "Yes" or "No"—is the best response. If your child can respond with great enthusiasm, that's even better. If your child is relaxed and comfortable beforehand, he'll be fine enough for the opening exchange of conversation before the actual audition begins. Mom and Dad, don't coach your child with silly dialogue. Behind closed doors, children will reveal what's been coached. It's better to make your child feel comfortable and allow conversation to flow from his little minds.

If your child is not taking acting lessons, help him practice his emotions at home. He should know how to reproduce such emotions as happiness, sadness, disappointment, silliness, as well as such abstract emotions as pensiveness, listlessness, etc.

Your child must be able to sparkle effortlessly, however it will take him a few times before he can put all of these exercises to practice. Your child

These photos of brothers were shot nearly 25 years ago. They would still work today.

will learn to channel his energy and use it to his favor at every interview.

Callback procedures are identical to those at the first audition. You'll sign in your child, help him rehearse his lines, and wait for his name to be called. Then, he'll meet with the casting people (and, perhaps the director) and read his lines. The main difference between first calls and callbacks is the time spent with the casting director. If he is in and out, this is not a good sign. If he is kept longer than the previous child, it's a better sign. If he is in with casting for a substantially longer time, the situation is quite positive. If the casting director says something to you, it's an excellent sign. Casting will not shake your hand and announce that he was hired; after all, your child isn't the only one on this call-back. But, you can be optimistic if the casting director asks your child to stay while she looks at some other kids, after which she brings him in again to have one more quick look at him. But, this still doesn't mean he booked the job. No matter how friendly casting may be to your or your child, he doesn't book the job until his agent is notified.

AFTER THE CALLBACK

After your child has completed the callback and has been released by casting, he will be returned to you in the waiting area and you will be free to go home. Don't be disappointed if there is no reaction from casting. Even if they loved him, they keep their emotions in check.

Don't make your child insane with a lot of questions; typically, he'll be noncommittal. However, he might be excited and want to tell you every detail, but don't count on it. And don't press for more and forget the "third degree." He might end up hating the whole audition process, thinking he'll never be able to satisfy you.

If the callback went well, usually you can tell immediately after the casting door opens. If your child is smiling or still partially conversing with the casting people, or if everyone inside comes out laughing or smiling, you can assume that the callback went well.

– NOTES –

– NOTES –

15
The Booking

After the callback, it's agony waiting for the phone to ring with the news that your child has booked the job. Somebody, (maybe even several somebodies) liked your child so much he wanted to see your little guy again. Right now, your child's chances are as good as anybody else's!

The casting director may ask for your child's availability. Commonly called "avail," this is a process used to place an actor on hold—for a specific time period and for a particular role—before the final selection is made. There are many reasons for placing an actor on avail. For instance, if a production company has not secured a shooting schedule, it will place the actors on avail for a short period of time, ensuring the actor's availability for the entire shooting schedule. Or, the creative people involved can't decide which direction to go with the casting: blondes or brunettes, girls or boys, eight-year-olds or ten-year-olds? The top choices in each category will be placed on avail until the final decision is made. (This often happens when casting tries to match child actors to parent actors.) Once the final decision has been made, the actors not selected will be released while the selected actors will be booked.

Being placed on avail and <u>not</u> booking the job is a disappointment, but cheer up: it means your child was the favorite in his category. (There will come a time when your child will be placed on avail and <u>will</u> book the job!) Availability can be annoying but it is a common courtesy agents and actors afford to producers and it happens frequently. The best way to look at it is as a third call.

KEEPING YOUR COOL

Oh, the anxiety . . . when will the agent hear something? How long will that be? You may hear quickly or, it may take two or three weeks. And, don't worry. If your child doesn't book the job, you will hear about that, too. Your child's agent will know who was cast as soon as the job is booked. If your child is the lucky one, you'll hear from your agent immediately.

So relax. There's nothing you can do until you receive that call.

Just when you think you'll never hear a word, the phone will ring and this time it will be different. You won't hear a typical "Hello;" instead, you'll hear someone happily report, "Congratulations! He booked it!" Oddly, you'll find yourself reacting calmly. You should be celebrating, right? But when you think about it, the stark reality is, your child is going to <u>work</u> and he'll be the one dancing on the ceiling. If that doesn't invoke a plethora of mixed emotions in you, it should! Your child is going to be on a set with the director, producer, crew members, and, he is going to be right in the middle of it all.

THE TAFT-HARTLEY

The first job for any actor in the business (child or adult) is worked under the "Taft-Hartley" law, which

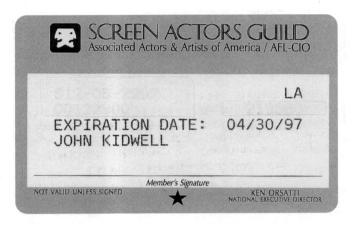

EXPIRATION DATE: 04/30/97
JOHN KIDWELL

LA

Member's Signature

NOT VALID UNLESS SIGNED

KEN ORSATTI
NATIONAL EXECUTIVE DIRECTOR

Sample SAG Card.

allows him to work one job before requiring him to join the union, because joining an actor's union (either SAG or AFTRA) is expensive. Currently it costs about $1,200. The current SAG scale for a day's pay is $443.25 for one day of a commercial shoot. Do the math. Therefore, if an actor works once and

never again, forcing him to join a union would deter many other actors from entering the business. The Taft-Hartley saves new actors from having the pay expensive initiation fees and annual dues for nothing. However, if an actor is over four years old, he has thirty days after working his first SAG job within which to officially join SAG. He may also work other SAG jobs during this time. After the thirty-day period, he must join SAG before working his next SAG job. The only exception is for children under the age of four who may work unlimited number of jobs before joining the union. Which union your child must join depends on the project he is hired for: AFTRA for television and commercials, or SAG for theatrical and television motion pictures projects and also for television and commercials. He will not be required to join both unions at the same time for the same job. Nearly all productions today fall under the jurisdiction of SAG, but at some point in a successful career, an actor will belong to both, and perhaps a handful of other unions as well. Although there are other actors unions, for the purposes of this book, we are concerned with the television and motion picture unions and SAG and AFTRA are the two main unions for this area of the business.

THE NEGOTIATIONS

Before your child actually goes to work (the period known as "principal photography"), the agent will negotiate his salary, dressing facilities and whatever other points she deems are important for your child.

If your child's first job is a commercial, his pay could be scale ($443.25 per day) or "scale plus ten," meaning $443.25 for the day's pay plus

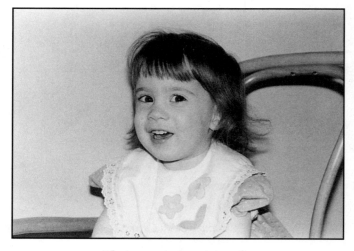

What every actor strives for.

10 percent (or $44.32) to cover the amount of the agent's commission. (It is rarely more than SAG scale for commercial work.) Residuals keep commercial pay scales low. Remember, while daily or

weekly salaries are better for films, commercials pay residuals every time the commercial is shown. The final amount can be staggering (especially if it's a national commercial shown in prime time), impressive (if it's a regional spot), or mediocre (for cable, buy-out or wildspots). The Federal Communications Commission tracks all commercials, so don't worry. If your child is owed residuals, he will get them.

If your child has been cast as the lead in a film, his salary paid could be scale plus ten for a weekly player, or if he is good enough to have a high-powered agency represent him, he could earn significantly more. Your child's agent will not set the deal without your approval. If you want to know what union rates are for various projects, call or write SAG or AFTRA; the union will send you a wage list for a small fee.

PRIOR TO THE SHOOT

Before your child is called to work, you will hear from various people connected with principal photography, including your child's agent, who will give you many details about the job. For example, the wardrobe people will need your child's sizes and will set up a wardrobe fitting if necessary. You may get a call from a production assistant to advise you of a change of location or call time. (The term "location" refers to the place where the filming of the job will be done. "On location" is used in when principal photography takes place away from your town.

If your child is cast in a film, he will have to visit a doctor for a check-up before starting. The producer's office will provide you the name and telephone number of the physician who is performing the examinations for all the actors. You will have to book an appointment and take your child there;

the production company will pay for the visit.

In all likelihood, you will have to take your child on a wardrobe call a day or two print to his first day of shooting to have him fitted for his costumes. If it is a contemporary movie, TV show or commercial, the wardrobe people may ask you to bring some of his own personal clothes: nothing fits a child as well as the clothes he normally wears. They will ask you to bring a couple of pairs of his shoes, too. Parents, this is a good time to caution you to try buying some of your child's clothes and shoes without names, advertising designs or logos on them. So, when bringing your child's clothes to the wardrobe people, try to bring generic-looking items, unless Wardrobe is specific about what they want you to bring.

You should also be thoroughly familiar with your child's wardrobe. For instance, you may be asked if he owns a sweatshirt with holes in it, or a red shirt or a battered pair of jeans; you should know whether or not he does. There are no wrong answers, only accurate ones. The wardrobe people are only trying to determine what clothing they may need to purchase for the shoot. (By the way, if your child wears his own clothes, he's compensated for them with a small fee above his daily rate—$15 per costume change for non-evening wear, $25 per costume change for evening wear and $10 for dancer's footwear.) Also, Mom and Dad, please make sure you know his correct size—from dress suits to sneakers to bathing suits! The wardrobe people buy the sizes you say your child wears; if you don't know, call them back after you measure him.

At the wardrobe call, you'll probably meet other crew members besides the wardrobe people. You should be able to learn a little more about the project (i.e., the exact locations, indoors, outdoors).

THE DAY OF THE SHOOT

Finally the day arrives! If your stomach feels like a pit (and you're nervous), hopefully you're not transferring your nerves to your child! He should be cool, relaxed and ready to have fun at work. A calm attitude generates a great response from all the adults your child will work with. Mom and Dad, you both should be gracious and pleasant. Don't forget to have a good time.

Let your child's agent talk you through a typical day of shooting. Don't be afraid to ask questions.

For the sake of this chapter, let's say your child has booked a one-day commercial shoot.

If your child attends school and school is in session, you must ask his teacher to prepare classwork and homework for him to complete while "in school" on the set. Even though it's only a one-day shoot, if school is in session, every school-age child under eighteen, must spend four hours of every workday in school. The social worker or studio teacher on the set to help him complete it. All children from infancy through eighteen years of age need a social worker/studio teacher on the set at all times while shooting. The social worker/studio teacher will grade your child's work that he completes on the set and give him a record of those grades to return to his school so he may get credit for his work and his attendance. These grades are averaged into his classroom grades and count on his report card. Your child should know this process so he won't slack off when attending school on the set. In the beginning, your child may think he's exempt from furthering his education, but he's not. Sometimes, the child is still in the classroom at the end of a long day of shooting working to make the required hours of school before he is allowed to leave for the day. Remember, if his grades slip below the standard required by your state, his work permit will not be renewed and he will not be able to work again until those grades improve.

WHAT SHOULD YOU EXPECT?

If your child knows what to expect, his first day of work will run smoothly; if he does not, it can be a disaster. On the first call and on the callback, your child was interviewed for several minutes. Now that he has been hired, he will be required to stand in front of the camera for as long as fifty minutes at a time, saying the same dialogue and performing the same actions over again until the director is satisfied with the scene. There are many reasons why "takes" don't come out perfectly. For example, noise levels and natural weather conditions can affect the number of takes necessary, especially when filming outdoors (e.g., airplanes going by overhead; car horns beeping; an unexpected flock of honking geese flying by; the sun dipping behind a cloud and ruining the light). An adorable kid may look charmingly spontaneous in that cereal commercial, but the truth is, that child was filmed over and over again, saying the same dialogue and eating yet another bite of cereal until he got it just right.

Work in this industry can be tedious, especially for young children. Forewarn your child about how the business works and how many times he (or another actor) may need to perform a single action in order to please the director. It gets more difficult when there are several people in the scene.

All directors like quiet on the set. This is crucial when cameras are rolling but it applies between takes as well. Parents, this includes you, too. Even whispering can ruin a scene or break the director's concentration. You will see the importance of this when your child films an outdoor scene: there is only so much daylight, so rather than risk interruptions from uncontrollable events or traffic noises, the director would prefer to get his take and move on.

Therefore, it is exceedingly important to be mindful of your surroundings. If your child is not on camera, it is your job to make sure he doesn't ruin it for the people who are!

WHAT TO DO TO MAINTAIN THE SPARKLE

Your child must sparkle and keep that sparkle fresh throughout the tedium of filming. That's easy to manage. There are several things your child should do daily to ensure he maintains his energy.

★ Sleep. He should get a good night's rest before every working day.

★ Eat. Your child should eat something before leaving the house. Even if it is only a light snack, he needs something to sustain him on the ride to work. All meals are provided by the production company coinciding with the hours of the shooting schedule. If your child's call is for early in the morning, breakfast is provided. Once you arrive at the set, however, your child may get called into makeup and or wardrobe, or just be too excited to eat. Once you get going, no one knows when the directors will call for a break, so it's important that he have some food in his stomach before arriving.

★ Bathe. Sounds silly, doesn't it? Your child should talk a bath and wash his hair every day. The wardrobe and hair people will appreciate it!

★ Exercise. While on the set, make sure your child takes the time to run around a little in between takes. It will help him work off a little steam and keep his circulation pumping. The social worker will find a safe area to do this. Any kind of exercise (jumping jacks, running, hopping) is important especially when he is in school on the set. During the school year, a child actor can go from hours of studying to perhaps an hour standing in front of the camera. He'll be expected to "sparkle" on cue for take after take. Therefore, keeping your child alert and relaxed

is critical. Just don't let him get out of control!

★ Sweets. Keep him away from too much sugar which does <u>not</u> give him the energy he needs.

★ Attitude. Keep your conversations with him on a positive note. Don't criticize his performance; the director will talk to him about his work. Inform your child as to what a director is and what his job entails. Make sure your child listens to the director and does what is asked of him. Most industry professionals are sensitive to children's needs and abilities. A well-behaved, easily-directed child is a delight to everyone who works with him.

You will hear horror stories from everyone who has worked with children about how exhausting a process it can be. Make sure that negative rumors don't start flying about your child. You will know immediately how his co-workers feel about him. Problems can be avoided if your child is well-behaved and prepared. Crew members will like him and will happily take the time to talk with him and explain how certain equipment works or why things are done a particular way. It can be a splendid experience for everyone if your child is enjoying himself and executing his responsibilities. However, if your child is difficult, every day of this shooting schedule will be long and dissatisfying.

Your child's first job should be viewed as an excellent learning experience. Don't be intimidated by not knowing everything that is expected of you or your child. He is not going to be asked to do anything that the director feels he won't or can't accomplish. (After all, your child auditioned for this part and got it, remember? Odds are, he knows more than you think he does.) In any case, he will have received his lines or a copy of the script, so he should be prepared for the work that is required of him. Now, your child only has to repeat his lines again and again until the director yells "Cut."

Once the director is happy with your child's day of performances, and if your child has finished the required time in the schoolroom, the two of you will be thanked and released. Once you sign him out, you both are free to go home.

STUNT REQUESTS

There are certain things you should not allow your child to do unless they were agreed upon previously by you and your agent. Don't let your child do anything dangerous! For example, you might arrive on the set one day to discover that the director has just decided to shoot your child swimming in a pool with real alligators. This is a NO, NO! Do not approve this action for your child! This is for the stunt people. Also, you should not let your child attempt an action just because he thinks he can do it. Any out-of-the-ordinary request should be reported immediately to the set social worker and to your child's agent.

WHO GETS THE CHECK

If your child was cast in a film, the producer will probably have hired a payroll company to process the payroll for the cast and crew. At any rate, your child's check will be sent to his agent. (When you signed with the agency, you were asked to sign "payroll authorizations" for the agency, allowing them to receive his paychecks. These forms allow the agent to endorse your child's checks and deposit them into the agency's bank account.) The agent then deducts her ten percent commission from the

gross amount and sends you a check, together with a copy of the work stub, for the balance. (Residuals are processed the same way.)

Save all of your child's payroll stubs. You will need them if he works enough days to become eligible for unemployment.

POST-PRODUCTION

Your child's job is over, but the producers are scurrying about with technicians in "post-production," editing the scenes together, adding special effects, sound effects (sweetener), music, etc., or otherwise preparing the project for release or airing.

DUBBING/LOOPING

Sometimes, after filming is completed, your child may be asked by the producers to go to a sound studio where he will re-speak his lines onto an audio track which then replaces the original spoken track. This process of "looping" often is necessary on large-scale productions, on exterior shots, or even if the director wants a line changed after the scene is shot and is compensated for above and beyond what was paid for the principal photography of the job. (It is easier—and less expensive— to delete the existing voice and re-record the actor onto the sound track than it is to set up another day of principal photography.)

When the project is completed, you may receive a videocassette copy of your child's work from the production company or ad agency; you may have to pay, however. Be sure to ask the producer while you're still on the set and people know your child. Film production companies spring up and disappear all the time, so don't count on being able to get a copy of your child's work if you wait too long. (You may also want to ask your agent if this can be included in your deal.)

– NOTES –

16
Managing Your Child's Money

Whether your child is working occasionally or his name and face have become familiar in the industry, you will face money-managing issues. We will focus on what the career of the "working child actor," not a "star" child actor whose needs are different and probably more complex. Whether your child is working regularly or sporadically, he is still referred to as a working actor. The information in this chapter is meant to clarify the issues connected with a working child actor's money.

OKAY, LET'S START WITH—WHO'S MONEY IS IT?
In case you don't realize it, your child's earnings, from his first day of work, belong to him. Your job is to safeguard his earnings until he reaches maturity, age eighteen, and then, hand the money over to him. However, you are entitled to something (after all, you helped him get this far); even his agent gets ten percent. The fact is, this amount varies. But, if you are doing this strictly for your child, you should give it all to him.

If you are not careful, managing your child's money can be the most difficult part of his career.

You may be thinking that your child would never have gotten this far without you, so why are you not allowed to spend his money freely. If you orchestrated his career simply to support you and your family, you would be accused of slave labor. After all, he's a minor and all rules concerning child labor laws apply to him as an actor the same way they apply if you got him a job working at McDonald's and you cashed his check every week.

Now that your child is working, you must manage a more hectic daily schedule and you must also consider his well-being and future. The entire family, in fact, will feel the pressure of the industry.

If he reaches the point in his career when he books one out of five or ten jobs, you might want to consider hiring a manager for him. Yes, Mom or Dad, you can manage his career early on, but once your child is earning six figures and is facing multiple film offers, it's better for him—and for you—to hand his career over. Don't fret: you won't be forgotten or ignored—you are the parents! There's no need to get down in the dirt with the negotiators. We feel it's best for the parents and the child to remain the good guys. After all, no one can agree to an offer of employment on your child's behalf without your consent. Why not remain the rational person who listens to advisors (agents and managers) and simply says "yes" or "no," to the offer. A good manager will charge you 5 to 20 percent of your child's earnings (most charge 15 percent and, yes, that is in addition to the 10 percent going to the agent). It's a lot of money to subtract from any paycheck, but it may be worth it: let someone else do the running around, phone calling, negotiating, etc. Then your only concern will be keeping your child well-balanced, rational and happy.

HOW DO YOU ACCOUNT FOR WHAT YOU SPEND? There are very strict regulations governing child actors and their earnings instituted to protect what rightfully is earned by the child. You'd be astonished at how the easy access to your child's money can get the best of you, and how you could—one day—find yourself going to great lengths to guarantee he keeps working to keep the money coming in.

How do you control your child's income? First, open a trust account in the his name using one or both parents, as guardian or trustee for the child. The child's social security number must be used on the account. Deposit his income in this account

As the "investor" in your child's career (after all, you paid for his photos, used gasoline in your car driving him to auditions, expended time and energy preparing him every step of the way), you are allowed to be reimbursed from your child's earnings. The State permits a reasonable amount of money to be returned to the parent, if the claims can be substantiated. These reimbursable expenses are above and beyond the managing fee, if the parent also manages his child's career. In addition, a parent may take a "guardian" salary from five to fifteen percent from his child for being on the set while his child is filming. After all, every child actor is required by law to have a legal guardian present on the set when he is filming, and his parent is the most logical choice. So, like any other job, the parent would receive a salary. However, there are regulations concerning this kind of fee, so check with your child's tax accountant before signing on to be a salaried employee of your child. The most important covenant concerning your child's income is to <u>responsible</u> where you child's earning are concerned!

KEEPING RECEIPTS AND LEDGERS

Keep accurate records of all expenses incurred while fostering your child's career. You should also secure the services of an entertainment accountant. (You should not determine what is and is not deductible unless accounting is your trade.)

Keep a ledger and collect receipts. You'll be helping your accountant at tax time. And, you may need the records if you are called into court in the future by your child to prove where his money has been spent. (Yep, it can happen, even to you.)

THE COOGAN LAW

Many parents, unfortunately, have spent their children's earnings supporting themselves and their families. In fact, it happened so frequently that "The Coogan Law" was passed regulating the use by parents of their children's earnings.

The Coogan Law is named for child actor Jackie Coogan who filed against his parents for misappropriating the money he earned. (When Coogan reached the legal age of eighteen, he asked his parents for the money he earned as a child actor. He then learned that his parents had spent every last dime! He was so upset that the took them to court and sued them for the missing funds.) Therefore, The Coogan Law protects moneys earned by minors in the industry working under court-approved contracts.

A court-approved contract is one that has been brought before a court by the producer, who asks the judge to review its terms and render a binding decision on (or "approve") the terms and conditions between the producer and the minor. At the same time the contract is approved, the court will create a trust or bank account (in the child's name) to be used in conjunction with the child's earnings on that particular project. Twenty-five percent of the child's net income from this project (or more, at the judge's sole discretion) is set aside in this account, which the child can legally take possession of when he turns eighteen. (This does not apply to his commercial earnings, only to theatrical work which has a court-approved contract.)

WHAT IS DEDUCTIBLE

Don't forget to file your child's taxes as soon as he begins earning income. What are fair reimbursable deductions he may claim? You must be able to prove that the expense was necessary to the well-being or advancement of his career. Unlike most other professions, actors can deduct many expenses that ordinary people cannot. Some of these deductions include, movie tickets, books about act-

ing (including trade publications like *The Hollywood Reporter, Variety* or *Dramalogue*), classes in drama, voice, music, dance, horseback riding, roller blading, sky diving; the agent and manager's commissions; his hair cut; videotapes or records; the telephone bill; union dues; special wardrobe; etc.

We know of one situation when a mother of a child actor was asked by wardrobe to bring two of his suits, one of which would be used. The mother purchased the suits specifically for the job; one was white, and the other maroon. These were expensive and the child refused to wear them after the project was over, so she deducted the cost of both suits on the child's income tax. Deducting the two suits caused the tax board to audit the account. The mother then had to explain the reason for the deduction. The audit board understood and allowed the deductions. When the time comes for your child to file taxes, your accountant will know what to do.

As a parent, you are empowered to deduct what you have spent on your child's career, but only with proper documentation.

Your highest priority as a guardian of your child's earnings should be saving it for him. He will sacrifice a great deal in order to be successful, often missing many activities that occur during normal childhood. By the time he's grown, he should have something to show for his hard work and sacrifices.

– NOTES –

– NOTES –

17
Unemployment

Once your child has earned the required amount of wages for the stated period of time (as per the Employment Development Department in his state) he is eligible to collect unemployment between jobs. Unlike all other unemployed individuals, actors are not always required to list the jobs they have interviewed for during the week in order to collect their weekly benefits. This is because the out-of-work actor is not responsible for his own employment (he must have an agent set up auditions for work, which is a service that the unemployment office is unable to provide). As in any other case, all moneys collected during unemployment must be declared on your child's taxes, along with his annual income.

For now, your child is operating under the same regulations as you, another employed individual. When your child files for unemployment, _he_ signs the card, not you! When he files his taxes, _he_ signs the returns, not you! Of course, all financial matters should be discussed with him openly and honestly—it's his money.

18

Who's Responsible For The Money?

You are the parent, thus, you are responsible for your child's earnings, so you must be very careful when making investments on his behalf. If you gamble on an investment and lose, you, then, are responsible for the loss, plus interest! (Again, keep careful records of all transactions.) If, for example, you buy property for him, he is the legal owner of it. Money invested in real estate on your childs behalf is still your responsibility and if the investment turns sour, you are still responsible.

At one point, the State of California tried to intervene and become the legal guardian for all children in the industry. This, of course, meant that parents or guardians would no longer be in control of their children's money. The parents of child actors organized, hired several high-profile attorneys and fought this action in the courts—and won. However, California once again will intervene if mishandling of children's earnings by their parents becomes a serious problem once again.

If your family should face an economic hardship, you may take another 5 percent to 10 percent above your managing fee. However, you must keep careful records so it can be proven later, if a dispute should arise.

Parents, whenever you have questions about your child's earnings, contact his agent, accountant, guild (SAG, AFTRA, etc.), the Labor Board, or any other actor-related association for answers.

Under no circumstances should your child work until he reaches the age of maturity and have nothing to show for it.

– NOTES –

– NOTES –

19

When To Call It A Day

As in all endeavors, there is the possibility of calling it a day, when the people involved should take stock and, perhaps, abandon the dream. Deciding when to jump off the merry-go-round takes courage. After all, you and your child wanted this career. You dreamed and sacrificed for him; you invested money, time and energy; how can you think of quitting?

Listen to your child. Sometimes your child's voice gets lost in the hub-hub. As a responsible parent, you must make a conscientious effort to listen to your child when he's ready to call it a day.

Believe him when he tells you he's had enough. It is possible to force him into continuing, but you may find his name all over the tabloids as a result. Don't risk your child's future.

When should you abandon the dream? If you're sensitive and aware, you'll know when the party's over. Watch your child. Has he lost his charm? Is he now more difficult than delightful? If his attitude and behavior seem to be headed in a downward spiral, it's time to quit. If he tells you to your face that he's tired of working, it's time to quit.

TAKING A BREAK

Be aware that there's is difference between a child who is ready to throw in the towel and one who needs a break. As his parent, you alone are qualified to appraise his mood. Sometimes, a month or two off is all it takes; if acting in his blood, he'll soon be asking to get back out there.

If he's really ready to quit, the first sign to you, Mom and Dad, will probably be on the set, in front of the cast and crew! When your child is difficult this way, remember that you are the parent; he's the child. The pressures of being a working child sometimes get the best of children. In the real world, it could be over something as elementary as doing homework or chores or taking a bath. In the world of entertainment, your child's temperament is being taxed on a daily basis.

Are you having to lay down too many rules? Are you having to bribe him more? Is he becoming demanding? Are you and your child not having fun? If these scenarios sound familiar, something is wrong. You're making matters worse by keeping an unhappy child (or his parent) in the industry. If you continue struggling to keep him in the industry, you'll have hell to pay later. Long after your child's career is over (and it will be, because very few child actors continue the profession into adulthood), the monster you created is still part of your life and your family. It's better in the long run to get him out of the spotlight and back into normalcy while you still have some control. "Lifers" in this business (i.e., Jodie Foster, Ron Howard, Drew Barrymore, Michael J. Fox) are few and far between. Working child actors rarely become tired of the work if their parents are doing their part.

You should have a standard of behavior that

you expect from your child. If he starts to misbehave, a serious talk between you—away from others—should end the problem. Remember to keep a sense of humor; most children revert to their natural dispositions with a little humorous coaxing. If you handle the situation calmly and correctly, the crew will forgive and forget. After all, adult actors throw temper tantrums, too, and their careers usually survive.

If he is having problems and it's early in his career, we suggest you give him a break. Hopefully, you will identify his difficulties before his career accelerates. Because after a child attains a certain amount of success, the decision to pull him out of the business is difficult often impossible to achieve. You may start to have second thoughts about his continuing in the business, but what if he's signed to a long-range project or TV series? It is compli-

cated and difficult to extricate your child from his studio contract.

QUITTING

However, if your child's transformation into a demon occurs more often and for longer periods of time, seriously consider removing him from the industry. You should also speak to your child's agent, most of whom are good judges of a child's "phase," opposed to a "new personality." (If your child has problems on a shoot, the agent will hear about it from others.) If he sincerely wants to continue his career, he will quickly straighten out his behavior.

In fairness to the child actor, any child who is cooped up on a set all day and not allowed a normal day of study and play, can suffer greatly; nothing you say will appease his anxiety. From his perspective, there is only one scenario: he's being tortured and you don't care. Therefore, monitor your child's emotions carefully; remember to keep lines of communications open; when he has a day off, make it a real day off—no talk about work! (If you promised him a day at Disneyland and his agent calls with an audition, go to Disneyland, unless it's a callback or a producer's meeting.)

A good way to see if your child has lost his zest for work is to offer to take him out of the business. Then, watch his reaction. If he smiles and leaps for joy, it's time for him to quit. On the other hand, if he hates the idea and asks for another chance, tell him he must straighten out his behavior or you will have no other choice but to pull him out.

— NOTES —

20

What Else Is There Besides Films, TV and Commercials?

While SAG represents professional actors and performing artists working in motion pictures, television and TV commercials, the guild also represents those who work in interactive multimedia productions, infomercials, industrial and educational films, student and experimental films, and music videos. SAG's members work as principal performers, voice-over performers, singers, dancers, voice-over performers, puppeteers and models.

NONUNION WORK

There are many nonunion projects that could give your child experience in front of the camera (i.e., nonunion industrial or educational films, documentaries, game shows, home videos, or even nonunion theatrical films). But, remember: nonunion credits do not help union actors. At the beginning of your child's career, they will help in assessing his acting potential. And, such a job could result in a nice piece of film for his reel that could make the difference between landing or not landing a good agent.

PRINT WORK
Like beauty pageants, print work (modeling) might earn your child some money, but it is also discounted when it comes to credits for his resume. Large print ads—the kind you see on posters or billboards—usually star children who have had lots of prior experience. However, depending on where in the country you live, print work can be satisfying, economically and emotionally.

VOICE-OVERS
Doing a voice-over is great work and it counts on your child's resume. In fact, performing voice-overs is some of the most sought-after work in the business, because it can be very lucrative.

EXTRA WORK
We don't suggest never allowing your child to work as an extra. However, it is sometimes very difficult to make the transition from SEG to SAG. It's fun for those who do not wish for careers as principal actors, or for those who want to brag about being in a movie. It is usually not a stepping stone to SAG work; it is a stepping stone to more extra work.

– NOTES –

– NOTES –

21
Generally Speaking

You now possess more information than most people who already have children in the business. The process of breaking a child into the industry appears more difficult on paper than it actually is. In fact, it can be similar to purchasing a piece of furniture you assemble yourself: when you first read the instructions, they're confusing. However, once you begin to assemble the item, one step at a time—you manage to put it together. As a review, we've encapsulated some of the more important points of our book.

FURTHERING YOUR CHILD'S CAREER

Let your agent lay the groundwork. The parent cannot speed up the process by sending pictures to casting directors or trying to contact them by phone. Unsolicited photos generally are tossed because they don't have the time to review pictures unless they are requested of agents for a specific project. You'll wind up using pictures that you will need on future calls, and you'll be spending unnecessarily on stamps and packaging. In addition, no casting person will accept or return a call from the parent of an unknown child actor. Imagine what their days would be like if they accepted calls from the parent of every child actor in the industry! If you insist on calling, casting will not hesitate to pick up the phone and complain to your child's agent. In fact, you will ruin any chance your child may have had with that casting person. Nobody likes pushy stage mothers or fathers!

CHANGING HIS IMAGE

Don't worry about your child's immediate lack of success. And, don't try to change his image because he hasn't achieved success yet; no one knows what audiences are going to like. Most times, success in the industry comes to those who won't give up; also you can't discount blind luck (i.e., being in the right place at the right time). Your child's natural abilities are his assets. No other child has them.

Therefore, your child's "comfort zone" must be protected at all times; he must always feel that he is right for the job because he is himself.

Discourage your child from mimicking other children he sees on calls. Always encourage him to be himself. Allow his natural personality to shine through if you want him to be as relaxed as possible.

MAINTAINING HIS INTEREST

How can you keep your child "up" and "on?" It's a matter of consistency. Below are some basic rules for you and your child to review every chance you can. (It's important for you and your child to be reminded of the commitment he is taking on.) Post the list where you both will see it.

BASIC RULES FOR THE CHILD ACTOR
Take good care of yourself.
Study hard.
Listen to your agent.
Listen to your parents.
Listen to your director.
Eat healthful snacks.
Exercise.
Enjoy what you're doing.
Keep your sense of humor.

BASIC RULE FOR THE PARENT
Listen to your child.

MAINTAINING HIS HEALTH
Take good care of your child. He should take his vitamins and eat healthy meals and snacks! He should get plenty of rest, especially when he's shooting. (He'll get a little cranky and tired when he's been on his feet for several hours, at the beck and call of his director.) He'll receive a ten-minute break every hour while shooting, but having to stand in one place for fifty minutes, or having to do twelve takes of the same scene can exhaust him.

Your child should have a healthy snack prior to an audition (that means no candy or foods containing a lot of sugar like sodas). Natural fruit juices are an ideal energy builder.

He should exercise or play everyday, even if it's only for a few minutes between takes. Don't be worried about him hurting himself or knocking out a tooth. Relax and let them play. Your child's social worker/studio teacher will help you fit such a period into his schedule. He was once a regular kid, remember? Let him be one whenever possible.

ON BEING SMART

He should study hard and get good grades. The one common denominator for all working child actors is their high level of intelligence. He can spend all day learning dialogue for the next day only to discover that all the dialogue has been changed—which is common—and he's got twenty minutes to learn his new lines so the production won't fall behind schedule. And, he'll most likely receive new blocking and directing instructions to learn.

ON LISTENING

Listen to your child's agent. She is your life line to the inner circle of the business. She knows what kind of children are hot and booking jobs and why. She is your child's inspiration because she has faith in him. If she didn't, she wouldn't be representing him.

Your child should listen to you. He is in the business because of his talent and desires; most show-business kids will tell you they always thought about being in the industry. But, he didn't get there alone. He owes a lot to his parents. He should be kind to you; his love for you should be obvious. If it's not, something is wrong. You, too, should frequently let him know how much you love him.

Your child should listen to his director, the person in charge on the shoot. No matter how big or small the part, the director should always be respected. And, remember: the director is the best person to have on your child's side.

Mom and Dad, listen to your child when he speaks. Where he ends up in life depends greatly on what you've taught him about himself and the world. Tell him you love him—often—and help him believe it by showing him your love and respect. Your child deserves all the love he can get from you.

ON BEING "NORMAL"
Your child should enjoy his work. He'll have the opportunity to go places and do things that many others only dream about. Parents, take lots of photographs. They're wonderful for the scrapbook.

Parents and children should keep a sense of humor! Take time out for giggling and squirming your hearts out, which is the best healer and mood elevator in any business. Find humor with every hard knock; you'll be surprised what it can do for the spirit and the mind!

IN CONCLUSION
We know we've been tough giving you information about the industry's expectations of you and your child, but it's a tough business and you will be happier in the long run knowing what to expect rather than having it hit you blindly.

This book is not intended to discourage any parent from entering his child into show business. In fact, we know that discouraging anyone from entering the industry is an impossibility, once he's made up his mind to do so.

Remember: your child's agent is his key into the industry; whenever and wherever there are problems or concerns, ask his agent.

The world of show business can be a wonderful place for a child actor who possesses talent and understands the pressures involved. We hope that after reading our book, you and your child have an increased awareness of the child actor's trials and tribulations as well as insight into what to expect from the industry. You do not face an easy road, but it's one that is well worth taking.

We wish you the best of luck and success with your child's career. As they say in show business . . . **break a leg!**

List Of Helpful Aids

Daily Planner—SAG sells one for about $5.00.

List of SAG Agencies—beginning on Page 207.

Trade Papers—These can be ordered by phone and mailed to you daily (Monday—Friday). They are tax deductible.

The Hollywood Reporter: 213-525-2150,
Daily Variety: 213-857-6600.

Phone Book—Your own, not the Yellow Pages. This is where you will put all your industry contacts.

Map Book—You must know exactly where you're going every time you get in your car.

Work Permit—Keep a copy of your child's permit in your daily planner. File the original in a safe place.

Social Security Card—Keep your child's number handy at all times.

Highlighter—Keep one in this book and another in your daily planner. A highlighter will help when trying to read lines with your child, when keeping track of important names and numbers, etc.

Scenes

We have written several scenes and monologues for you to practice with your child, depending on his age. We have tried to include something for everybody.

The age ranges for each scene are only general and any child can read any part that might appeal to him. Where there are two people in a scene and you only have one child, Mom or Dad should play the other character.

"Rejection"

Two-person scene—Robert: 12-14—Cindy: 12-14.

Robert stands center stage. He is watching Cindy sitting at a table eating her lunch and reading a book. Robert then heaves a heavy sigh and turns to the audience.

ROBERT

There she is.
(he points to Cindy)
Over there. That's Cynthia Lewis. She's only the most awesome creature on the planet . . . and talk about brains. She's got brains comin' out of her ears . . . well, not literally, of course. But she's smart. Look at her. She's totally rad, isn't she? The problem is, she's so perfect, I can't seem to get up the nerve to talk to her. And I really need to talk to her. Our school is having this dance in two weeks and I want to ask her if she'll go with me, but every time I get near her, I get all freaked out and my breathing gets short and then I start to hyperventilate and before I know it, someone is reviving me in the nurse's office. It's a nightmare.
(Pause)
I know it's all in my head, of course. She just has me psyched I mean, I realize that all I have to do is walk up to her and say, "Hey, Cindy. I was wondering if you'd like to go to the dance with me?" I mean, what could she possibly say that would be so terrible? I've asked around and so far she's not going with anyone.

He looks over at Cindy and then faces the audience.

ROBERT (CONT'D)

Look at her. She's probably just sitting there waiting for me to come up to her and ask her to go . . . so why can't I do it?

(beat)

It's not like I haven't had the opportunity. We've got four classes together this year. Four whole classes. I sit right next to her for one of them. It makes me feel happy and sick to my stomach at the same time. That's four classes, five times a week, forty weeks out of the year and I still haven't said one word to her. I'm a loser.

He looks over at Cindy and then faces the audience.

                    ROBERT (CONT'D)
Did I mention I'm afraid of rejection? I don't know why but I'm sure that's my problem. I don't know what it is I think she would do to me. Look at her. She's so totally cool, she wouldn't hurt a fly. What am I so hung up about?
          (determined)
That's it! I've had enough! I'm going to do it! I'm just going to walk up to her and ask her to go to the dance with me. I'll just walk right up to her.
          (he doesn't move)
As soon as I catch my breath.

He lays a hand on his chest to steady himself.

                    ROBERT (CONT'D)
Okay. That's better. Here I go.

He turns to face her. He confidently walks over to her. He clears his throat. Cindy looks up from her book. She smiles. Robert smiles.

                    ROBERT (CONT'D)
Hey, Cindy, I was wondering if you'd like to go to the dance with me next Friday.

The smile fades from Cindy's face.

                    CINDY
Drop dead, Robert!

Robert staggers backwards as Cindy returns to her book. Robert faces the audience.

                    ROBERT

That was worse than I thought. I can't believe
she said that. "Drop dead." Did you hear it?
"Drop dead!" Why would she say that? I'm not a
bad person. I'm not a person who would do
unkind things to anyone. I'm thoughtful. I'm
cool. I'm hip. And I'm clean. I got an A in
Health and Hygiene last semester to prove it.

He is suddenly indignant.

                    ROBERT (CONT'D)

You know what I think? I think that was cold.
No, rude. That was very rude of her. Making a
comment like that with no explanation. I've got
a good mind to go back to her and tell her to
"drop dead."

In disbelief, he grabs the side of his head with his
hands.

                    ROBERT (CONT'D)

What am I saying?
                    (beat)
I know, I'll go back and ask her why she said
that.

He clears his throat and tucks in his shirt neatly.

                    ROBERT (CONT'D)

Here I go. I'm doing it now.

He walks back to the table. Cindy looks up from her
book. She smiles. Robert smiles.

                    CINDY

Yes, Robert?

                    ROBERT

Cindy, I was just wondering, you know . . .
what you said earlier? What was it? Oh, yes,
drop something or other . . well, I was
wondering, why exactly you would say something
like that to me? Have I done something to
offended you?

                    CINDY

Well, Robert, I would say something like that
to you so you would know, without a shadow of a
doubt, that I wouldn't go any place with you,
at any time, for any reason, if you were the
last living, breathing thing on the planet.

Robert just stares at her for a moment as she smiles at him.

                    ROBERT
              (beat)
     Oh.

     I see.

Robert walks back to center stage and faces the audience.

                    ROBERT (CONT'D)
     How humiliating! She really does want me dead!
     That's terrible. My heart is going to stop
     beating inside my chest. I don't think I'll
     live to see another sunrise. What would be the
     point?
              (pause)
     On the other hand, Mary Baker is kinda awesome.
     Maybe I'll ask her to go to the dance with me.

He walks offstage.

"Saying Good-bye"

Best friends Rachel and Janice are 9-11 years old. They have lived next door to each other since they were three. Janice is moving away and Rachel has come to say good-bye. Janice sits on the steps of the porch.

            RACHEL

Hi.

            JANICE

Hi.

            RACHEL

Your dad said you'd be leaving in a couple minutes, so I thought I'd say good-bye.

Janice turns away from her.

            JANICE

See ya.

Rachel joins her on the porch.

            RACHEL

Hey, it's not that bad.

            JANICE

Yes, it is. I'm never gonna see you again.

            RACHEL

Yes, you will. You're moving, not dying. Besides, my mom promised every summer we'll come and visit.

            JANICE

Parents always say that. It never happens.

            RACHEL

Yeah, but it's different with us.

            JANICE

Suppose you make new friends and you don't think about me anymore? Then what?

            RACHEL

Jan, nobody could ever replace you. Not ever.

Janice turns to her.

            JANICE

You mean it?

RACHEL
We're best friends, remember?

JANICE
What are we gonna do?

RACHEL
We could write all the time.

JANICE
I hate writing letters.

RACHEL
Well, when I'm thirteen, my mom said I could have my own phone. Then we could talk on the phone all the time.

JANICE
You won't be thirteen for two years!

RACHEL
I have patience.

Janice looks at her for a moment and then she smiles.

JANICE
Yeah. You do.

They hug.

RACHEL
Well, I'd better let you go.

JANICE
Yeah. I gotta get my stuff.

Rachel stands. Janice stands, too.

RACHEL
So . . . .

JANICE
So . . . .

RACHEL
I'm sure gonna miss you.

JANICE
I'm gonna miss you, too.

The two girls burst into tears and throw their arms around each other. They release and wipe their tears.

RACHEL
I wasn't gonna cry.

JANICE
I won't tell anyone if you don't.

                    RACHEL

          It's a deal.

She extends her hand. They shake on it. Rachel smiles
and starts to leave.

                    JANICE

          Rachel?

Rachel turns around to face her.

                    RACHEL

          Yeah?

                    JANICE

          If you write me, I promise I'll write back. I
          swear.

Rachel smiles.

                    RACHEL

          I'll check the mail everyday.

                    JANICE

          Don't worry, I won't let you down.

                    RACHEL

          You never have. That's why you'll always be my
          best friend.

They stare at each other for a long time and then suddenly, without a word, Rachel turns to go home and
Janice turns to go into her house.

"The Brain and the Brawn"

The scene takes place in the waiting room of the Principal's office. Mike (the school jock) and Doug (the school Einstein) sit in chairs next to each other. They are 13-15 years old. Mike looks at Doug.

                    MIKE

Hey, whadda ya know. Mr. Douglas-big-brains Ryan. What are you doing in here?

Doug doesn't look at him.

                    DOUG

If you have to know, I'm getting a note sent home to my parents.

                    MIKE
               (shocked)
You're kidding? Me, too! What are you flunking?

                    DOUG

Flunking?

                    MIKE

Yeah, you know like in the big "F." Wait, don't tell me. You're failing health. Or Phys Ed. Am I right?

                    DOUG

Hardly. I'm getting a note of congratulations sent to my parents for perfect attendance and for making the honor roll.

                    MIKE

Oh . . . .

                    DOUG

And you?

                    MIKE

Me?

                    DOUG

Why are you here?

                    MIKE

I'm getting a letter sent home, too.

Dough looks at him with surprise.

195

DOUG
Really?

MIKE
Yeah. They want to make sure my parents are disappointed because I turned the gas on the bunsen burner and then looked for a match. When I lit it, it caused a large explosion.

DOUG
That was you?

MIKE
Yeah.

DOUG
Wow. The whole school is talking about it.

MIKE
So what's the big deal. Nobody was hurt.

DOUG
Lucky for you.

MIKE
That's the only reason they didn't expel me. That and the fact that I'm the only guy on the baseball team who can hit one over the fence.

DOUG
The coach won't even let me try out for the team.

MIKE
Why would a guy like you wanna play sports?

DOUG
What do you mean, "a guy like me"?

MIKE
Well, you know. You're kind of . . .

DOUG
Nerdy?

MIKE
Yeah, that's it. Nerdy.

DOUG
Yeah, well, it just so happens, I got a great arm.

MIKE
For what?

DOUG
Pitching, that's what!

                    MIKE
          Okay, okay. Don't get your feathers ruffled.

Mike looks at Doug carefully, as if he's studying him
for a moment.

                    MIKE (CONT'D)
          You know, maybe we could help each other out,
          here.

                    DOUG
          What do you mean?

                    MIKE
          Well, I'd be willing to put in a word with the
          coach, if you'd be willing to . . .

Mike looks around to make sure nobody overhears him.

                    MIKE (CONT'D)
          . . . if you'd be willing to sort of, you
          know, tutor me in a couple of things.

                    DOUG
          I'd do anything to try out for the team. What
          subjects are you having trouble in?

                    MIKE
          English and science . . . and geography . . .
          and history.

                    DOUG
          You're flunking four classes?

                    MIKE
          Not flunking. Floundering. Is it a deal or not?

Doug thinks it over for a moment. He's leery.

                    DOUG
          How do I know your talking to the coach would
          do me any good.

                    MIKE
          Are you kidding? I put in a word, you're prac-
          tically on the team. You said you got a great
          arm, didn't ya?

Doug thinks about it again. A huge smile floods his
face. He extends his hand to shake. Mike smiles, too, as
they shake.

                    DOUG
          You got yourself a deal.

                    MIKE
          But if you tell anybody, I'll have to kill ya.

197

DOUG
Of course. It's understood.

Both satisfied, the boys return to silence.

"Twins"

Carol and Karen, 5- to 6-year-old twins, are playing on the floor of their bedroom with their dolls. Karen is combing her doll's hair; Carol is dressing her's.

                    CAROL

    Karen?

                    KAREN

    What?

                    CAROL

    What do you want to be when you grow up?

                    KAREN

    I dunno. Married, I guess. Like Mommy.

                    CAROL

    No, I don't mean like that. I mean like what
    kind of work do you want to do?

                    KAREN

    Work?

                    CAROL

    Yeah, you know. Like, when I grow up, I wanna
    be a doctor and take care of people.

                    KAREN

    Oh, I get it.

She thinks for a moment.

                    KAREN (CONT'D)

    Well, if you're going to be a doctor, I guess
    I'll be a patient.

                    CAROL

    You can't be a patient.

                    KAREN

    Why not? Lots of people are patients.

                    CAROL

    You can't make money at it, that's why!

                    KAREN

    Why not?

                    CAROL

    You are so stupid sometimes. Patients don't get
    paid for being sick.

KAREN

They don't?

CAROL

When Mommy takes you to the doctor, do they pay you?

Karen thinks about it for a moment.

KAREN

No.

CAROL

You have to pick something else.

KAREN

Okay, then I think I'll be married and do laundry and make the beds.

CAROL

You can't make money at that either!

KAREN

So?

CAROL

So, how're you gonna pay for things?

KAREN

I don't know. Maybe you could give me some of your money.

CAROL

I'm not giving you any of my money. Being a doctor is hard work. I'm gonna keep it for myself.

KAREN

I'd give you some money if you didn't have any.

Carol looks at her sister for a moment.

CAROL

You would?

KAREN

Sure.

She shows her doll to Carol.

KAREN (CONT'D)

How does she look?

CAROL

Great.

KAREN

Hey, you know what? I could be a designer. They make more money than doctors.

CAROL

Yeah! Then I wouldn't have to be a doctor.

KAREN

Why not?

CAROL

'Cause you just said you'd give me some of your money, right?

KAREN

Oh, yeah. Right.

Karen puts her doll down.

KAREN (CONT'D)

I don't want to play this anymore. Let's go ride bikes.

Carol puts down her doll, too.

CAROL

Okay. But this time, I get to give you the ticket.

KAREN

No way. It's my turn.

CAROL

Is not!

KAREN

Is too!

The two girls exit as they continue to argue.

"Grounded"

Betsy is 8-11 years old. She has just been grounded for teasing her little sister.

BETSY

How come I always get blamed? Huh? Would somebody like to tell me? Everything's always my fault. Nothing's ever Jessica's fault, 'cause she's only five and when you're five nobody ever thinks you do anything bad. Especially when they have a ten-year-old named Betsy to blame stuff on! Like the other night, I was supposed to be watching TV with Jessie, and I was, and everything was going really good, and then this really scary movie came on. Well, Jessie started to scream, but I thought that meant she liked it, 'cause it made me scream too, so we just kept watchin'. Then Dad came into the room and got really mad, because he said I should have known better than to let Jessie watch such a scary program. Anyway, he grounded me. For a week. Why don't they just kill me and get it over with? I mean, big deal, so we watched ten minutes of The Night Of the Living Dead. So, what?! Besides, I don't know what the big deal is about protecting Jessie. Jessie wasn't the only one who had nightmares. I haven't been able to sleep for a week. Even now I think those dead guys might be watching me from under the porch. Sometimes, I think I can hear them breathing outside my window at night . . . real heavy and slow and really dead like . . .

She shudders.

BETSY (CONT'D)

. . . but then, nothing ever happens and then I get mad 'cause I remember I'm grounded and there's not really any walking dead people to be afraid of. And I remember why I'm grounded. All because of Jessica. It's not fair. I get blamed for everything!

She walks off.

"Siblings"

Scene for two children. Jill, 11-14 and Joey, 6-8. Joey sits on the floor watching his sister putting on makeup. He frowns.

JOEY

Aren't you afraid you'll go blind with all that gook on your eyes?

Jill tries to make light of his comment.

JILL

You're just jealous.

JOEY

What's that supposed to mean?

JILL

You're just jealous because there's nothing boys can do to improve their appearance. They're stuck with what they were born with.

He gets up and goes to the mirror and peers in behind her.

JOEY

Are you saying I'm a dog.

JILL

Well, let's face it, Joey. You're no Rhett Butler.

JOEY

Who's that?

JILL

See? That's just what I'm talking about. You're stuck.

JOEY

You know, I think all that hair spray you've been usin' has seeped to your brain!

He goes back to his comic book on the floor.

JILL

Why don't you go bother Mom?

JOEY

'Cause she went to the market. She told me to come and bother you 'til she gets back.

                    JILL
        Well, then, that makes me in charge. And if I'm
        in charge, I command you to sit on the floor
        and be quiet.

                    JOEY
        Yeah? I'd like to see you try and make me.

        She reaches in her pocket and takes out a dollar. She
        extends it to him. He takes the dollar, puts it in his
        pocket and goes back to reading his comic.

        Jill puts the finishing touches on her makeup. Brushes
        her hair. Puts her brush down and looks at herself
        admiringly in the mirror.

                    JILL (CONT'D)
        There. Absolute perfection.

        Joey looks up from his comic. Jill looks down at him.

                    JILL (CONT'D)
        If you say one word, I'm taking back the dol-
        lar.

        Joey thinks for a moment and goes back to his comic.
        Jill smiles at herself in the mirror.

SAG Advice Regarding Agents

SAG offers the following advice to all actors who are looking to secure representation from an agency.

1. Make sure your agent is franchised with SAG before signing an agency contract or accepting verbal representation.

2. Agent's client lists are available to SAG members for inspection at the SAG's Agency Department.

3. All changes in your SAG agency listing must be made in writing - we cannot accept them by phone. Always include your Social Security number.

4. "Verbal" contracts (where there is no written agency contract in existence, or while new contracts are being prepared) can be filed with SAG by the performer, by sending SAG a written letter stating that they are represented by XYZ talent agent, or XYZ filed for representation; or by the Talent Agent using the Client Confirmation Form. This information will remain in SAG's computer system until we are advised, in writing, to remove and/or change the information.

5. Improper behavior by an agent should be reported to SAG immediately. These matters are handled confidentially. Your name is never used without your consent.

6. SAG does not have jurisdiction over print work and/or modeling work.

7. With respect to all monies for TV and Theatrical compensation, the agent has three (3) business days from the time the agency receives the money; and with respect to monies received as compensation for television commercials, five (5) business days from the time the agent receives the money from the employer. Commencing November 21, 1990, for payments received from an employer drawn on a financial institution located in a state other than the state in which the agent's office is located, the time for the agent to pay over to the actor shall be extended to seven (7) calendar days.

8. Make sure that you are using the SAG form contract when signing with an agency, and never sign contracts that contain blank spaces or are missing information.

9. SAG does not regulate Personal Managers.

SAG Talent Agents

All Guild members' talent agents must be franchised by the Guild. Following is a complete national list of all talent agents currently franchised by SAG (dated, May 1997); if any information is incorrect, please notify your local SAG office. Following the agent's telephone number is the type of representation offered by the agency.

This information franchise reflects only that the agent or agency is state-licensed where required; it has provided a surety bond or other security; it has submitted recommendations from people in the industry; and has promised to comply with SAG's rules governing agents and agencies.

The granting of a franchise by SAG does not in any manner, directly or indirectly, constitute a guarantee, warranty or representation as to an agent's ability or quality, or the conduct of the agent toward a performer. The SAG franchise does not indicate whether complaints have been filed with SAG against the agent or agency. Under confidentiality requirements, the SAG franchise does not reflect whether the Guild has initiated any proceeding to discipline or revoke the franchise of the talent agency or agency.

Los Angeles Area

ASA
4430 Fountain Ave., Suite A
Los Angeles, CA 90029
213-662-9787
Full Service

ABOVE THE LINE AGENCY
9200 Sunset Blvd., Suite 401
Los Angeles, CA 90069
310-859-6115
310-859-6119
Full Service

ABRAMS ARTISTS & ASSOC.
9200 Sunset Blvd., Suite 625
Los Angeles, CA 90069
310-859-0625
Full Service

ABRAMS-RUBALOFF & LAWRENCE
8075 West Third. St., Suite 303
Los Angeles, CA 90048
213-935-1700
Full Service

ACME TALENT & LITERARY, TALENT AGENCY
6310 San Vicente Blvd., Suite 520
Los Angeles, CA 90048
213-954-2263
Full Service

AGENCY FOR PERFORMING ARTS
9000 Sunset Blvd., Suite 1200
Los Angeles, CA 90069
310-273-0744
Full Service

THE AGENCY
1800 Ave. of the Stars, Suite 400
Los Angeles, CA 90067
310-551-3000
Full Service

AIMEE ENTERTAINMENT
15000 Ventura Blvd., Suite 340
Sherman Oaks, CA 91401
818-783-9115

ALLEN TALENT AGENCY
11755 Wilshire Blvd., Suite 1750
Los Angeles, CA 90025
213-896-9372

ALLIANCE TALENT INC.
9171 Wilshire Blvd., Suite 441
Beverly Hills, CA 90210
310-858-1090

CARLOS ALVARADO AGENCY
8455 Beverly Blvd., Suite 406
Los Angeles, CA 90048
213-655-7978

AMBROSIO/MORTIMER
9150 Wilshire Blvd., Suite 175
Beverly Hills, CA 90212
310-274-4274
Full Service

AMSEL, EISENSTADT & FRAZIER
6310 San Vicente Blvd., Suite 401
Los Angeles, CA 90048
213-939-1188

ANGEL CITY TALENT
1680 Vine St., Suite 716
Los Angeles, CA 90028
213-463-1680

IRVIN ARTHUR ASSOC.IATES LTD
9363 Wilshire Blvd., Suite 212
Beverly Hills, CA 90210
310-278-5934

ARTIST.MANAGEMENT AGENCY
4340 Campus Drive, Suite 210
Newport Beach, CA 92660
714-261-7557

ARTIST.NETWORK
8438 Melrose Place
Los Angeles, CA 90069
213-651-4244

ARTISTS AGENCY
10000 Santa Monica Blvd., Suite 305
Los Angeles, CA 90067
310-277-7779
Full Service

ARTISTS GROUP, LTD
10100 Santa Monica Blvd., Suite 2409
Los Angeles, CA 90067
310-552-1100
Full Service

ATKINS AND ASSOC.IATES
303 S. Crescent Heights
Los Angeles, CA 90048
213-658-1025

BADGLEY & CONNOR
9229 Sunset Blvd., Suite 311
Los Angeles, CA 90069
310-278-9313
Full Service

BAIER-KLEINMAN INTERNATIONAL
3575 West Cahuenga Blvd., Suite 500
Los Angeles, CA 90068
818-761-1001

BALDWIN TALENT, INC.
1640 5th St., Suite 201
Santa Monica, CA 90401
310-899-1166
Full Service

BOBBY BALL TALENT AGENCY
4342 Lankershim Blvd.
Universal City, CA 91602
818-506-8188
Full Service

BAUMAN, HILLER & ASSOC.IATES
5757 Wilshire Blvd., Penthouse 5
Los Angeles, CA 90036
213-857-6666
Full Service

SARA BENNETT AGENCY
6404 Hollywood Blvd., Suite 327
Los Angeles, CA 90028
213-965-9666
Full Service

BENSON, LOIS
8360 Melrose Ave., Suite 203
Los Angeles, CA 90069
213-653-0500

MARION BERZON TALENT AGENCY
336 East 17th St.
Costa Mesa, CA 92627
714-631-5936

BONNIE BLACK TALENT AGENCY
4660 Cahuenga Blvd., Suite 306
Toluca Lake, CA 91602
818-753-5424
Full Service

THE BLAKE AGENCY
415 N. Camden Drive, Suite 111
Beverly Hills, CA 90210
310-246-0241

J MICHAEL BLOOM AND ASSOCIATES
9255 Sunset Blvd., 7th Floor
Los Angeles, CA 90069
310-275-6800
Full Service

NICOLE BORDEAUX TALENT AGENCY
616 N. Robertson Blvd., 2nd Floor
Los Angeles, CA 90069
310-289-2550
Commercials

BORINSTEIN ORECK BOGART
8271 Melrose Ave., Suite 110
West Hollywood, CA 90046
213-658-7500

BRAND MODEL AND TALENT
17941 Skypark Circle, Suite F
Irvine, CA 92714
714-850-1158
Full Service

PAUL BRANDON & ASSOC.
1033 N. Carol Drive, Suite T-6
Los Angeles, CA 90069
310-273-6173

BRANDON'S COMMERCIALS UNLIMITED, S.W.
9601 Wilshire Blvd., Suite 620
Beverly Hills, CA 90210
310-888-8788
Full Service

KELLY BRESLER & ASSOCIATES
15760 Ventura Blvd., Suite 1730
Encino, CA 91436
818-905-1155

DON BUCHWALD & ASSOCIATES
9229 Sunset Blvd.
Los Angeles, CA 90069
310-278-3600
Full Service

BURKETT TALENT AGENCY
12 Hughes, Suite D-100
Irvine, CA 92718
714-830-6300
Full Service

IRIS BURTON AGENCY
1450 Belfast Drive
Los Angeles, CA 90069
310-652-0954
Child Actors
Full Service
Commercials
Young Adults

C LA VIE MODEL AND TALENT
7507 Sunset Blvd., Suite 201
West Hollywood, CA 90046
213-969-0541
Full Service

CL INC.
843 N. Sycamore Ave.
Los Angeles, CA 90038
213-461-3971

CNA & ASSOCIATES, INC.
1925 Century Park East, Suite 750
Los Angeles, CA 90067
310-556-4343
Full Service

CACTUS TALENT AGENCY
13601 Ventura Blvd., Suite 112
Sherman Oaks, CA 91423
818-986-7432
Full Service

BARBARA CAMERON & ASSOCIATES
8369 Sausalito Ave., Suite A
West Hills, CA 91304
818-888-6107
818-888-6172
Child Actors
Full Service

CAPITAL ARTISTS
8383 Wilshire Blvd., Suite 954
Beverly Hills, CA 90211
213-658-8118

CAREER ARTISTS INTERNATIONAL
11030 Ventura Blvd., Suite 3
Studio City, CA 91604
818-980-1315
Full Service

WILLIAM CARROLL AGENCY
139 N. San Fernando Rd., Suite A
Burbank, CA 91502
818-848-9948
Full Service

CASTLE-HILL TALENT AGENCY
1101 S. Orlando Ave.
Los Angeles, CA 90035
213-653-3535
Full Service

CAVALERI & ASSOCIATES
405 South Riverside Drive, Suite 200
Burbank, CA 91506
818-955-9300
Full Service

CENTURY ARTISTS, LTD
9744 Wilshire Blvd., Suite 308
Beverly Hills, CA 90212
310-395-3800
Full Service

THE CHARLES AGENCY
11950 Ventura Blvd., Suite 3
Studio City, CA 91604
818-761-2224
Full Service

THE CHASIN AGENCY
8899 Beverly Blvd., Suite 716
Los Angeles, CA 90048
310-278-7505

CHATEAU BILLINGS TALENT AGENCY
5657 Wilshire Blvd., Suite 340
Los Angeles, CA 90036
213-965-5432
Full Service

JACK CHUTUK & ASSOCIATES
10586 Cheviot Drive, Suite 700
Los Angeles, CA 90067
310-552-1773

CINEMA TALENT AGENCY
2609 Wyoming Ave.
Burbank, CA 91505
818-845-3816
Full Service

CIRCLE TALENT ASSOCIATES
433 N. Camden Drive, Suite 400
Beverly Hills, CA 90212
310-285-1585
Full Service

W. RANDOLPH CLARK COMPANY
13415 Ventura Blvd., Suite 3
Sherman Oaks, CA 91423
818-385-0583
Full Service

COLLEEN CLER MODELING
120 S. Victory Blvd., Suite 206
Burbank, CA 91502
818-841-7943
818-841-4541
Child Actors
Full Service
Commercials
Theatrical

COAST TO COAST TALENT GROUP, INC.
4942 Vineland Ave, Suite 200
North Hollywood, CA 91601
818-762-6278
Full Service

COLOR ME BRIGHT
433 N. Camden Drive, Suite 400
Beverly Hills, CA 90210
310-858-1681
Full Service

COLOURS MODEL & TALENT MANAGEMENT AGENCY
8344-1/2 West Third St.
Los Angeles, CA 90048
213-658-7072
Full Service

CONTEMPORARY ARTISTS, LTD.
309 Santa Monica Blvd., Suite 304
Santa Monica, CA 90401
310-395-1800
Full Service

COPPAGE COMPANY, THE
11501 Chandler Blvd.
North Hollywood, CA 91601
818-980-1106

CORALIE JR. THEATRICAL AGENCY
4789 Vineland Ave., Suite 100
North Hollywood, CA 91602
818-766-9501
Full Service

THE COSDEN AGENCY
3518 West Cahuenga Blvd., Suite 216
Los Angeles, CA 90068
213-874-7200
Full Service

THE CRAIG AGENCY
8485 Melrose Place, Suite E
Los Angeles, CA 90069
213-655-0236

CREATIVE ARTISTS AGENCY, LLC
9830 Wilshire Blvd.
Beverly Hills, CA 90212
310-288-4545
Full Service

SUSAN CROW & ASSOCIATES
1010 Hammond St., Suite 102
Los Angeles, CA 90069
310-859-9784
Full Service

CUNNINGHAM, ESCOTT & DIPENE
10635 Santa Monica Blvd., Suite 130
Los Angeles, CA 90025
310-475-2111
Full Service

DH TALENT AGENCY
1800 N. Highland Ave., Suite 300
Los Angeles, CA 90028
213-962-6643
Full Service

DZA TALENT AGENCY
8981 Sunset Blvd., Suite 503
Los Angeles, CA 90069
310-274-8025
Full Service

DADE/SCHULTZ ASSOC.IATES
11846 Ventura Blvd., Suite 201
Studio City, CA 91604
818-760-3100

THE DEVROE AGENCY
6311 Romaine St.
Los Angeles, CA 90038
213-962-3040
Full Service

DURKIN ARTISTS
127 Broadway, Suite 210
Santa Monica, CA 90401
310-458-5377
Full Service

DYTMAN AND SCHWARTZ, TALENT AGENCY
9200 Sunset Blvd., Suite 809
Los Angeles, CA 90069
310-274-8844

ELITE MODEL MANAGEMENT
345 N. Maple Drive, Suite 397
Beverly Hills, CA 90210
310-274-9395
Full Service

ELLECHANTE TALENT AGENCY
274 Spazier Ave.
Burbank, CA 91502
818-557-3025
Full Service

ELLIS TALENT GROUP
6025 Sepulveda Blvd., Suite 201
Van Nuys, CA 91411
818-997-7447

ENDEAVOR TALENT AGENCY, LLC
350 S. Beverly Blvd., Suite 300
Beverly Hills, CA 90212
310-226-8500
Full Service

EPSTEIN-WYCKOFF & ASSOC.IATES
280 S. Beverly Drive, Suite 400
Beverly Hills, CA 90212
310-278-7222

ESTEPHAN TALENT AGENCY
6018 Greenmeadow Road
Lakewood, CA 90713
310-421-8048
Full Service

EXPRESS ENTERTAINMENT, TALENT AGENCY
3402 Macarthur Blvd., Suite D
Santa Ana, CA 92704
714-557-8423
Full Service

FPA, TALENT AGENCY
12701 Moorpark, Suite 205
Studio City, CA 91604
818-508-6691

EILEEN FARRELL/CATHY COULTER TALENT AGENCY
7313 Kraft Ave.
North Hollywood, CA 91605
818-765-0400
Full Service

FAVORED ARTISTS AGENCY
122 South Robertson Blvd., Suite 202
Los Angeles, CA 90048
310-247-1040

FERRAR-MAZIROFF ASSOC.IATES
8430 Santa Monica Blvd., Suite 220
Los Angeles, CA 90069
213-654-2601
Commercials

FILM ARTISTS ASSOCIATES
13563 Ventura Blvd.
Sherman Oaks, CA 91043
818-386-9669
Full Service

FIRST.ARTISTS AGENCY
10000 Riverside Drive, Suite 10
Toluca Lake, CA 91602
818-509-9292

FLICK EAST & WEST TALENTS, INC.
9057 Nemo St., Suite A
Los Angeles, CA 90069
310-271-9111
Full Service

JUDITH FONTAINE AGENCY, INC.
205 South Beverly Drive, Suite 212
Beverly Hills, CA 90212
310-275-4620
Commercials

BARRY FREED COMPANY
2029 Century Park East ,Suite 600
Los Angeles, CA 90067
310-277-1260

BRUCE FREUND TALENT AGENCY
23011 Moulton Parkway, Suite E-1
Laguna Hills, CA 92653
714-494-5934

ALICE FRIES AGENCY
1927 Vista Del Mar Ave.
Los Angeles, CA 90068
213-464-1404

FUTURE AGENCY
8929 S. Sepulveda Blvd., Suite 314
Los Angeles, CA 90045
310-338-9602
Full Service

GVA TALENT AGENCY, INC.
9025 Wilshire Blvd., Suite 301
Beverly Hills, CA 90210
310-278-1310
Full Service

GRA/GORDON RAEL AGENCY, LLC
9255 Sunset Blvd., Suite 404
Los Angeles, CA 90069
310-285-9552
Full Service

THE GAGE GROUP INC.
9255 Sunset Blvd., Suite 515
Los Angeles, CA 90069
310-859-8777
Full Service

HELEN GARRETT TALENT AGENCY
6435 Sunset Blvd.
Los Angeles, CA 90028
213-871-8707
Full Service

DALE GARRICK INTERNATIONAL
8831 Sunset Blvd., Suite 402
Los Angeles, CA 90069
310-657-2661

THE GEDDES AGENCY
1201 Green Acre Ave.
West Hollywood, CA 90046
213-878-1155

LAYA GELFF ASSOC.IATES
16133 Ventura Blvd., Suite 700
Encino, CA 91436
818-713-2610

PAUL GERARD. TALENT AGENCY
11712 Moorpark St., Suite 112
Studio City, CA 91604
714-644-7950

DON GERLER AGENCY
3349 Cahuenga Blvd., Suite 1
Los Angeles, CA 90068
213-850-7386
Full Service

THE GERSH AGENCY
232 N. Canon Drive
Beverly Hills, CA 90210
310-274-6611
Full Service

GOLD/MARSHAK/LIEDTKE & ASSOC.IATES
3500 West Olive Ave., Suite 1400
Burbank, CA 91505
818-972-4300
Full Service

GOLDEY COMPANY, INC.
116 N. Robertson Blvd., Suite 700
Los Angeles, CA 90048
310-657-3277

MICHELLE GORDON & ASSOC.IATES
260 S. Beverly Drive, Suite 308
Beverly Hills, CA 90212
310-246-9930
Full Service

GREENE & ASSOC.IATES
8899 Beverly Blvd., Suite 705
Los Angeles, CA 90048
310-288-2100

HWA TALENT REPRESENTATIVES, INC.
1964 West wood Blvd., Suite 400
Los Angeles, CA 90025
310-446-1313
Full Service

HAEGGSTROM OFFICE,TALENT AGENCY
6404 Wilshire Blvd., Suite 1100
Los Angeles, CA 90048
213-658-9111

BUZZ HALLIDAY & ASSOC.IATES
8899 Beverly Blvd., Suite 620
Los Angeles, CA 90048
310-275-6028
Full Service

HALPERN & ASSOC.IATES
12304 Santa Monica Blvd., Suite 104
Los Angeles, CA 90025
310-571-4488
Full Service

HAMILBURG AGENCY, MITCHELL J.
292 S. La Cienega, Suite 312
Beverly Hills, CA 90211
310-657-1501

VAUGHN D. HART & ASSOC.IATES
8899 Beverly Blvd., Suite 815
Los Angeles, CA 90048
310-273-7887

BEVERLY HECHT AGENCY
12001 Ventura Blvd., Suite 320
Studio City, CA 91604
818-505-1192
Full Service

HENDERSON-HOGAN AGENCY
247 South Beverly Drive, Suite 102
Beverly Hills, CA 90212
310-274-7815
310-274-0751
Full Service
Theatrical

HERVEY/GRIMES TALENT AGENCY
12444 Ventura Blvd., Suite 103
Studio City, CA 91404
818-981-0891
Full Service

HOLLANDER TALENT GROUP, INC.
3518 Cahuenga Blvd. West ,Suite 316
Los Angeles, CA 90068
213-845-4160
213-845-4170
Child Actors
Full Service
Commercials
Young Adults
Theatrical

HOUSE OF REPRESENTATIVES TALENT AGENCY
400 S. Beverly Drive, Suite 101
Beverly Hills, CA 90212
310-772-0772

HOWARD. TALENT WEST
11712 Moorpark St., Suite 205-B
Studio City, CA 91604
818-766-5300
Full Service

MARTIN HURWITZ ASSOC.IATES
427 N. Canon Drive, Suite 215
Beverly Hills, CA 90210
310-274-0240

IFA TALENT AGENCY
2049 Century Park East ,Suite 2500
Los Angeles, CA 90067
310-659-5522

INNOVATIVE ARTISTS
1999 Ave Of The Stars, Suite 2850
Los Angeles, CA 90067
310-553-5200
Child Actors
Full Service

INNOVATIVE ARTISTS YOUNG TALENT DIVISION
1999 Ave. of The Stars
Los Angeles, CA 90067
310-553-5200
Child Actors
Full Service

INTERNATIONAL CHILDREN'S AGENCY
4605 Lankershim Blvd., Suite 201
North Hollywood, CA 91602
818-755-6600
Child Actors
Full Service

INTERNATIONAL CREATIVE MANAGEMENT
8942 Wilshire Blvd.
Beverly Hills, CA 90211
310-550-4000
Full Service

IT MODEL MANAGEMENT
526 North Larchmont Blvd.
Los Angeles, CA 90004
213-962-9564
Full Service

JEOW ENTERTAINMENT, TALENT AGENCY
1717 N. Highland Ave., Suite 805
Los Angeles, CA 90028
213-468-9470
Full Service

JS REPRESENTS, TALENT AGENCY
509 North Fairfax Ave., Suite 216
Los Angeles, CA 90036
213-653-2577
Full Service

GEORGE JAY AGENCY
6269 Selma Ave., Suite 15
Los Angeles, CA 90028
213-466-6665
Full Service

THOMAS JENNINGS & ASSOC.IATES
28035 Dorothy Drive, Suite 210A
Agoura, CA 91301
818-879-1260
Full Service

THE KAPLAN-STAHLER AGENCY
8383 Wilshire Blvd., Suite 923
Beverly Hills, CA 90211
213-653-4483

KARG/WEISSENBACH & ASSOC.IATES
329 N. Wetherly Drive, Suite 101
Beverly Hills, CA 90210
310-205-0435

KAZARIAN/SPENCER & ASSOC.IATES
11365 Ventura Blvd., Suite 100
Studio City, CA 91604
818-769-9111
Full Service

KELMAN/ARLETTA
7813 Sunset Blvd.
West Hollywood, CA 90046
213-851-8822
Full Service

SHARON KEMP TALENT AGENCY
309 Santa Monica Blvd., Suite 401
Santa Monica, CA 90401
310-552-0011

KERWIN WILLIAM AGENCY
1605 N. Cahuenga Blvd., Suite 202
Los Angeles, CA 90028
213-469-5155
Full Service

TYLER KJAR AGENCY
10653 Riverside Drive
Toluca Lake, CA 91602
818-760-0321
Full Service

ERIC KLASS AGENCY
144 S. Beverly Drive, Suite 405
Beverly Hills, CA 90212
310-274-9169

PAUL KOHNER, INC.
9300 Wilshire Blvd., Suite 555
Beverly Hills, CA 90212
310-550-1060
Full Service

VICTOR KRUGLOV & ASSOC.IATES,
7060 Hollywood Blvd., Suite 1220
Los Angeles, CA 90028
213-957-9000
Full Service

LA TALENT
8335 Sunset Blvd., 2nd Floor
Los Angeles, CA 90069
213-656-3722
Full Service

LA ARTISTS
606 Wilshire Blvd., Suite 416
Santa Monica, CA 90401
310-395-9589

LW 1, INC.
8383 Wilshire Blvd., Suite 649
Beverly Hills, CA 90211
213-653-5700
Commercials

STACEY LANE TALENT AGENCY, STACEY
13455 Ventura Blvd., Suite 240
Sherman Oaks, CA 91423
818-501-2668
Full Service

CHIARINA LEE TALENT AGENCY
838 N. Fairfax Ave, Suite C
West Hollywood, CA 90046
213-957-2304
Full Service

LENHOFF/ROBINSON TALENT AND LIT. AGENCY
1728 S. La Cienega Blvd.
Los Angeles, CA 90035
310-558-4700

THE LEVIN AGENCY
8484 Wilshire Blvd., Suite 745
Beverly Hills, CA 90211
213-653-7073
Full Service

LEVY, ROBIN & ASSOC.IATES
9220 Sunset Blvd., Suite 303
Los Angeles, CA 90069
310-278-8748
Full Service

TERRY LICHTMAN CO
4439 Wortser Ave.
Studio City, CA 91604
818-783-3003

ROBERT LIGHT AGENCY
6404 Wilshire Blvd., Suite 900
Los Angeles, CA 90048
213-651-1777
Full Service

KEN LINDNER & ASSOC.IATES
2049 Century Park East ,Suite 2750
Los Angeles, CA 90067
310-277-9223

LOS ANGELES PREMIERE ARTISTS AGENCY
8899 Beverly Blvd., Suite 510
Los Angeles, CA 90048
310-271-1414
Full Service

LOVELL & ASSOC.IATES
7095 Hollywood Blvd., Suite 1006
Los Angeles, CA 90028
213-876-1560

JANA LUKER TALENT AGENCY
1923 ¹/₂ West wood Blvd., Suite 3
Los Angeles, CA 90025
310-441-2822
Full Service

LUND AGENCY/INDUSTRY ARTISTS TALENT AGENCY
3330 Barham Blvd., Suite 103
Los Angeles, CA 90068
818-508-1688

LYNNE & REILLY AGENCY
10725 Vanowen St., Suite 113
Toluca Plaza Bldg.
North Hollywood, CA 91605
213-850-1984
Full Service

MGA/MARY GRADY AGENCY
4444 Lankershim Blvd., Suite 207
North Hollywood, CA 91602
818-766-4414
Full Service

MADEMOISELLE TALENT AGENCY
8693 Wilshire Blvd., Suite 200
Beverly Hills, CA 90211
310-289-8005
Full Service

MAJOR CLIENTS AGENCY
345 Maple Drive, Suite 395
Beverly Hills, CA 90210
310-205-5000

MALAKY INTERNATIONAL
10642 Santa Monica Blvd., Suite 103
Los Angeles, CA 90025
310-234-9114
Full Service

ALESE MARSHALL MODEL & COMMERCIAL
AGENCY
23900 Hawthorne Blvd., Suite 100
Torrance, CA 90505
310-378-1223
Commercials

MAXINE'S TALENT AGENCY
4830 Encino Ave.
Encino, CA 91316
818-986-2946
Full Service

MEDIA ARTISTS GROUP
8383 Wilshire Blvd., Suite 954
Beverly Hills, CA 90211
213-658-5050
Full Service

METROPOLITAN TALENT AGENCY
4526 Wilshire Blvd.
Los Angeles, CA 90010
213-857-4500
Full Service

MIRAMAR TALENT AGENCY
7400 Beverly Blvd., Suite 220
Los Angeles, CA 90036
213-934-0700
Full Service

PATTY MITCHELL AGENCY
4605 Lankershim Blvd., Suite 201
North Hollywood, CA 91602
818-508-6181
Child Actors
Full Service
Commercials
Young Adults
Theatrical

WILLIAM MORRIS AGENCY
151 El Camino Dr
Beverly Hills, CA 90212
310-274-7451
Full Service

H DAVID MOSS & ASSOC.
733 North SewaRd. St., Penthouse
Los Angeles, CA 90038
213-465-1234

MARY MURPHY AGENCY
6014 Greenbush Ave.
Van Nuys, CA 91401
818-989-6076
Full Service

SUSAN NATHE & ASSOC.IATES/CPC
8281 Melrose Ave., Suite 200
West Hollywood, CA 90046
213-653-7573
Full Service

NEXT MANAGEMENT CO., TALENT AGENCY
662 N. Robertson Blvd.
Los Angeles, CA 90069
310-358-0100
Full Service

OMNIPOP INC.
10700 Ventura Blvd., Second Floor
Studio City, CA 91604
818-980-9267
Full Service

ORANGE GROVE GROUP, INC.
12178 Ventura Blvd., Suite 205
Studio City, CA 91604
818-762-7498

Your Kid Ought To Be In Pictures

CINDY OSBRINK TALENT AGENCY
4605 Lankershim Blvd., Suite 401
North Hollywood, CA 91602
818-760-2488
818-760-0991
Child Actors
Full Service
Commercials
Theatrical

DOROTHY DAY OTIS & ASSOC.IATES
373 South Robertson Blvd.
Beverly Hills, CA 90211
310-652-8855
Full Service

PAKULA KING & ASSOC.IATES
9229 Sunset Blvd., Suite 315
Los Angeles, CA 90069
310-281-4868

PARADIGM TALENT AGENCY
10100 Santa Monica Blvd., Suite 2500
Los Angeles, CA 90067
310-277-4400
Full Service

THE PARTOS COMPANY
6363 Wilshire Blvd., Suite 227
Los Angeles, CA 90048
213-876-5500

PERSEUS MODELING & TALENT
3807 Wilshire Blvd., Suite 1102
Los Angeles, CA 90010
213-383-2322
Full Service

PLAYERS TALENT AGENCY
8770 Shoreham Drive, Suite 2
Los Angeles, CA 90069
310-289-8777
Full Service

PRIVILEGE TALENT AGENCY
8170 Beverly Blvd., Suite 204
Los Angeles, CA 90048
213-658-8781
Full Service

PRO-SPORT & ENTERTAINMENT CO
11661 San Vicente Blvd., Suite 304
Los Angeles, CA 90049
310-207-0228
Full Service

PROGRESSIVE ARTISTS
400 S. Beverly Drive, Suite 216
Beverly Hills, CA 90212
310-553-8561

QUALITY ARTISTS
5455 Wilshire Blvd., Suite 1807
Los Angeles, CA 90036
213-936-8400
Full Service

RENAISSANCE TALENT & LITERARY AGENCY
8523 Sunset Blvd.
Los Angeles, CA 90069
310-289-3636

STEPHANIE ROGERS & ASSOC.
3575 West Cahuenga Blvd., Suite 249
Los Angeles, CA 90068
213-851-5155

CINDY ROMANO MODELING & TALENT AGENCY
414 Village Square West
Palm Springs, CA 92262
619-323-3333
Full Service

GILLA ROOS WEST LTD
9744 Wilshire Blvd., Suite 203
Beverly Hills, CA 90212
310-274-9356
Full Service

THE MARION ROSENBERG OFFICE
8428 Melrose Place, Suite B
Los Angeles, CA 90069
213-653-7383

SDB PARTNERS, INC.
1801 Ave. of the Stars, Suite 902
Los Angeles, CA 90067
310-785-0060

SAMANTHA GROUP, TALENT AGENCY
300 S. Raymond Ave., Suite 11
Pasadena, CA 91105
818-683-2444
Full Service

THE SANDERS AGENCY
8831 Sunset Blvd., Suite 304
Los Angeles, CA 90069
310-652-1119
Full Service

SARNOFF COMPANY, INC.
3900 W. Alameda Ave.
Burbank, CA 91505
818-972-1779

THE SAVAGE AGENCY
6212 Banner Ave
Los Angeles, CA 90038
213-461-8316
Full Service

JACK SCAGNETTI TALENT AGENCY
5118 Vineland Ave., Suite 102
North Hollywood, CA 91601
818-762-3871
Full Service

THE IRV SCHECHTER COMPANY
9300 Wilshire Blvd., Suite 410
Beverly Hills, CA 90212
310-278-8070
Full Service

SCHIOWITZ/CLAY/ROSE, INC.
1680 N. Vine St., Suite 614
Los Angeles, CA 90028
213-463-7300
Full Service

SANDIE SCHNARR TALENT
8500 Melrose Ave., Suite 212
Los Angeles, CA 90069
213-653-9479
Commercials

JUDY SCHOEN & ASSOC.IATES
606 N. Larchmont Blvd., Suite 309
Los Angeles, CA 90004
213-962-1950

DON SCHWARTZ ASSOC.IATES
6922 Hollywood Blvd., Suite 508
Los Angeles, CA 90028
213-464-4366
Full Service

SCREEN ARTISTS AGENCY
12435 OxnaRd. St.
North Hollywood, CA 91606
818-755-0026
Full Service

SELECTED ARTISTS AGENCY
3900 West Alameda Ave., Suite 1700
Burbank, CA 91505
818-972-1747
Full Service

SHAPIRA & ASSOC.
15301 Ventura Blvd., Suite 345
Sherman Oaks, CA 91403
818-906-0322
Full Service

SHAPIRO-LICHTMAN, INC.
8827 Beverly Blvd.
Los Angeles, CA 90048
310-859-8877

DOROTHY SHREVE AGENCY, DOROTHY
2665 N. Palm Canyon Drive
Palm Springs, CA 92262
619-327-5855

THE SHUMAKER TALENT AGENCY
6533 Hollywood Blvd., Suite 401
Los Angeles, CA 90028
213-464-0745
Full Service

JEROME SIEGEL ASSOC.IATES
7551 Sunset Blvd., Suite 203
West Hollywood, CA 90046
213-850-1275

SIERRA TALENT AGENCY
14542 Ventura Blvd., Suite 207
Sherman Oaks, CA 91403
818-907-9645
Full Service

SILVER,MASSETTI & SZATMARY/WEST LTD.
8730 Sunset Blvd., Suite 440
Los Angeles, CA 90069
310-289-0909
Full Service

RICHARD. SINDELL & ASSOC.IATES
8271 Melrose Ave., Suite 202
West Hollywood, CA 90046
213-653-5051

SIRENS MODEL MANAGEMENT
9455 Santa Monica Blvd.
Beverly Hills, CA 90210
310-246-1969
Commercials

MICHAEL SLESSINGER ASSOC.
8730 Sunset Blvd., Suite 220
Los Angeles, CA 90069
310-657-7113

SUSAN SMITH & ASSOC.IATES
121 N. San Vicente Blvd.
Beverly Hills, CA 90211
213-852-4777

CAMILLE SORICE TALENT AGENCY
16661 Ventura Blvd., Suite 400-E
Encino, CA 91436
818-995-1775
Full Service

SPECIAL ARTISTS AGENCY
345 North Maple Drive, Suite 302
Beverly Hills, CA 90210
310-859-9688
Full Service

STAR ATHLETE TALENT AGENCY
468 N. Camden Drive, 2nd Floor
Beverly Hills, CA 90210
310-285-1752
Full Service

CARYN STARLING TALENT AGENCY
10057 Riverside Dr., Suite 203
Toluca Lake, CA 91602
818-766-0436

STARWILL TALENT AGENCY
6253 Hollywood Blvd., Suite 730
Los Angeles, CA 90028
213-874-1239
Full Service

CHARLES H. STERN AGENCY
11766 Wilshire Blvd., Suite 760
Los Angeles, CA 90025
310-479-1788

STONE MANNERS AGENCY
8091 Selma Ave.
West Hollywood, CA 90046
213-654-7575
Full Service

PETER STRAIN AND ASSOC.IATES
8428 Melrose Place, Suite D
Los Angeles, CA 90069
213-782-8910
Full Service

SUN AGENCY
8961 Sunset Blvd., Suite V
Los Angeles, CA 90069
310-888-8737
Full Service

SUNSET WEST MODELS, TALENT AGENCY
8490 Sunset Blvd., Suite 502
Los Angeles, CA 90069
310-659-5340
Full Service

SUTTON, BARTH & VENNARI INC.
145 S. Fairfax Ave., Suite 310
Los Angeles, CA 90036
213-938-6000
Commercials

TALENT GROUP INC.
6300 Wilshire Blvd., Suite 2110
Los Angeles, CA 90048
213-852-9559
Full Service

TALON THEATRICAL AGENCY
567 South Lake
Pasadena, CA 91101
818-577-1998
Full Service

TANNEN & ASSOC.
8370 Wilshire Blvd., Suite 209
Beverly Hills, CA 90211
213-782-0515
Full Service

THOMAS TALENT AGENCY
6709 La Tijera Blvd., Suite 915
Los Angeles, CA 90045
310-665-0000
Full Service

ARLENE THORNTON & ASSOC.IATES
12001 Ventura Place, Suite 201
Studio City, CA 91604
818-760-6688
Commercials

TISHERMAN AGENCY, INC.
6767 ForeSt.Lawn Drive, Suite 101
Los Angeles, CA 90068
213-850-6767
Commercials

A TOTAL ACTING EXPERIENCE
20501 Ventura Blvd., Suite 399
Woodland Hills, CA 91364
818-340-9249
Full Service

TURNING POINT MGMT SYSTEM, TALENT AGENCY
6601 Center Drive West ,Suite 500
Los Angeles, CA 90045
310-348-8171
Full Service

THE TURTLE AGENCY
12456 Ventura Blvd., Suite 1
Studio City, CA 91604
818-506-6898

TWENTIETH CENTURY ARTISTS
15315 Magnolia Blvd., Suite 429
Sherman Oaks, CA 91403
818-788-5516
Full Service

UMOJA TALENT AGENCY
2069 W. Slauson Ave.
Los Angeles, CA 90047
213-290-6612
Full Service

UNITED TALENT AGENCY, INC.
9560 Wilshire Blvd., 5th Floor
Beverly Hills, CA 90212
310-273-6700
Full Service

VISION ART MANAGEMENT
9200 Sunset Blvd.
Penthouse 1
Los Angeles, CA 90069
310-888-3288

ERIKA WAIN AGENCY
1418 N. Highland Ave, Suite 102
Los Angeles, CA 90028
213-460-4224

WALLIS AGENCY
1126 Hollywood Way, Suite 203-A
Burbank, CA 91505
818-953-4848
Full Service

WARDLOW AND ASSOC.IATES
1501 Main St., Suite 204
Venice, CA 90291
310-458-1292

ANN WAUGH TALENT AGENCY
4731 Laurel Canyon Blvd., Suite 5
North Hollywood, CA 91607
818-980-0141
Full Service

RUTH WEBB ENTERPRISES
7500 Devista Drive
West Hollywood, CA 90046
213-874-1700
Full Service

SHIRLEY WILSON & ASSOC.IATES
5410 Wilshire Blvd., Suite 227
Los Angeles, CA 90036
213-857-6977
Full Service

WORLD CLASS SPORTS
880 Apollo St., Suite 337
El Segundo, CA 90245
310-535-9120
Full Service

WORLD WIDE ACTS, TALENT AGENCY
5830 Las Virgenes Road, Suite 492
Calabasas, CA 91302
818-340-8151
Full Service

CARTER WRIGHT ENTERPRISES
6513 Hollywood Blvd., Suite 210
Los Angeles, CA 90028
213-469-0944
Full Service

WRITERS AND ARTISTS AGENCY
924 West wood Blvd., Suite 900
Los Angeles, CA 90024
310-824-6300
Full Service

YBA ENTERPRISES, TALENT AGENCY
8380 Melrose Ave., Suite 311
Los Angeles, CA 90069
213-655-7245
Full Service

STELLA ZADEH & ASSOCIATES
11759 Iowa Ave.
Los Angeles, CA 90025
310-207-4114

ZEALOUS ARTISTS P., INC.
139 S. Beverly Drive, Suite 222
Beverly Hills, CA 90212
310-281-3533
Full Service

New York Area

ABRAMS ARTISTS & ASSOCIATES
420 Madison Ave., 14th Floor
New York, NY 10017
212-935-8980
Child Actors
Full Service

ACME TALENT & LITERARY AGENCY
625 Broadway, 8th Floor
New York, NY 10012
212-328-0387
Full Service

BRET ADAMS LTD.
448 West 44th St.
New York, NY 10036
212-765-5630
Full Service

AGENCY FOR PERFORMING ARTS
888 Seventh Ave., 6th Floor
New York, NY 10106
212-582-1500
Full Service

AGENCY FOR THE COLLABORATIVE ARTS, INC.
132 West 22nd St., 4th Floor
New York, NY 10011
212-807-8344

AGENTS FOR THE ARTS, INC.
203 West 23rd St., 3rd Floor
New York, NY 10011
212-229-2562
Full Service

ALLIANCE TALENT INCORPORATED
1501 Broadway, Suite 404
New York, NY 10036
212-840-6868
Full Service

MICHAEL AMATO THEATRICAL ENTERPRISE
1650 Broadway, Suite 307
New York, NY 10019
212-247-4456
Full Service

AMBROSIO/MORTIMER & ASSOCIATES
165 West 46th St., Suite 1214
New York, NY 10036
212-719-1677
Full Service

AMERICAN INTERNATIONAL TALENT
303 West 42nd St., Suite 608
New York, NY 10036
212-245-8888
Full Service

BEVERLY ANDERSON AGENCY
1501 Broadway, Suite 2008
New York, NY 10036
212-944-7773
Full Service

ANDREADIS TALENT AGENCY, INC.
119 West 57th St., Suite 813
New York, NY 10019
212-315-0303
Full Service

ARTIST'S AGENCY, INC.
230 West 55th St., Suite 29D
New York, NY 10019
212-245-6960
Full Service

ARTISTS & AUDIENCE ENTERTAINMENT
2112 Broadway, 6th Floor
New York, NY 10023
212-721-2400
Full Service

ARTISTS GROUP EAST
1650 Broadway, Suite 711
New York, NY 10019
212-586-1452
Full Service

ASSOCIATED BOOKING CORPORATION
1995 Broadway
New York, NY 10023
212-874-2400
Full Service

RICHARD ASTOR AGENCY
250 West 57th St., Suite 2014
New York, NY 10107
212-581-1970
Full Service

CAROL BAKER AGENCY
165 West 46th St., Suite 1106
New York, NY 10036
212-719-4013
Commercials

BARRY HAFT BROWN ARTISTS
165 West 46th St., Suite 908
New York, NY 10036
212-869-9310
Full Service

BAUMAN HILLER & ASSOCIATES
250 West 57th St., Suite 2223
New York, NY 10107
212-757-0098
Full Service

PETER BEILIN AGENCY
230 Park Ave., Suite 1223
New York, NY 10169
212-949-9119
Full Service

BETHEL AGENCY
360 West 53rd St., Suite BA
New York, NY 10019
212-664-0455
Full Service

BIG DUKE SIX ARTISTS AGENCY, INC.
5 Union Square West
New York, NY 10003
212-989-6927
Full Service

J MICHAEL BLOOM & ASSOCIATES
233 Park Ave. South, 10th Floor
New York, NY 10003
212-529-6500
212-529-5838
Child Actors
Full Service
Commercials
Young Adults
Theatrical

BOOKERS INC.
150 Fifth Ave., Suite 834
New York, NY 10011
212-645-9706
Full Service

226

DON BUCHWALD & ASSOC.
10 East 44th St.
New York, NY 10017
212-867-1070
Full Service

CARRY COMPANY
1501 Broadway, Suite 1410
New York, NY 10036
212-768-2793
Full Service

THE CARSON ORGANIZATION, LTD.
240 West 44th St., Penthouse 12
New York, NY 10036
212-221-1517
Full Service

CARSON/ADLER AGENCY, INC.
250 West 57th St., Suite 729
New York, NY 10107
212-307-1882
212-541-7008
Child Actors
Full Service
Commercials
Young Adults
Theatrical

RICHARD CATALDI AGENCY
151 West 46th St., Suite 1502
New York, NY 10036
212-819-0422
Full Service

CLASSIC MODEL & TALENT MANAGEMENT, INC.
87 South Finley Ave.
Basking Ridge, NY 7920
908-766-6663
Full Service

COLEMAN-ROSENBERG
155 E. 55th St., Apt. 5D
New York, NY 10022
212-838-0734
Full Service

CUNNINGHAM-ESCOTT-DIPENE & ASSOCIATES
257 Park Ave. South, Suites 900 & 950
New York, NY 10010
212-477-1666
Child Actors
Full Service
Commercials
Young Adults

GINGER DICCE TALENT AGENCY, INC.
1650 Broadway, Suite 714
New York, NY 10019
212-974-7455
Full Service

DOUGLAS, GORMAN, ROTHACKER & WILHELM, INC.
1501 Broadway, Suite 703
New York, NY 10036
212-382-2000
Full Service

DUVA-FLACK ASSOCIATES, INC.
200 West 57th St., Suite 1008
New York, NY 10019
212-957-9600
Full Service

DULCINA EISEN ASSOCIATES
154 East 61st St.
New York, NY 10021
212-355-6617
Full Service

EPSTEIN-WYCKOFF & ASSOCIATES
311 West 43rd St., Suite 304
New York, NY 10036
212-586-9110
212-586-8019
Child Actors
Full Service
Young Adults

FRONTIER BOOKING INTERNATIONAL, INC.
1560 Broadway, Suite 1110
New York, NY 10036
212-221-0220
Child Actors
Full Service
Commercials
Young Adults
Theatrical

THE GAGE GROUP INC.
315 West 57th St., Suite 4H
New York, NY 10019
212-541-5250
Full Service

GARBER AGENCY
2 Pennsylvania Plaza, Suite 1910
New York, NY 10121
212-292-4910
Full Service

THE GERSH AGENCY NEW YORK, INC.
130 West 42nd St., Suite 2400
New York, NY 10036
212-997-1818
Full Service

GILCHRIST TALENT GROUP, INC.
630 Ninth Ave., Suite 800
New York, NY 10036
212-692-9166
212-953-4188
Child Actors
Full Service
Commercials
Young Adults
Theatrical

HWA TALENT REPRESENTATIVES
36 East 22nd St.
3rd Floor
New York, NY 10010
212-529-4555
Full Service

PEGGY HADLEY ENTERPRISES, LTD.
250 West 57th St.
New York, NY 10019
212-246-2166
Full Service

HARDEN-CURTIS ASSOCIATES
850 Seventh Ave, Suite 405
New York, NY 10019
212-977-8502
Full Service

MICHAEL HARTIG AGENCY LTD.
156 Fifth Ave., Suite 820
New York, NY 10010
212-929-1772
Full Service

HENDERSON/HOGAN AGENCY INC.
850 Seventh Ave., Suite 1003
New York, NY 10019
212-765-5190
212-586-2855
Child Actors
Full Service
Young Adults
Theatrical

BARBARA HOGENSON AGENCY
19 West 44th St., Suite 1000
New York, NY 10036
212-730-7306
Full Service

INGBER & ASSOCIATES
274 Madison Ave., Suite 1104
New York, NY 10016
212-889-9450
Commercials

INNOVATIVE ARTISTS TALENT AND LITERARY AGENCY
141 5th Ave., 3rd Floor
New York, NY 10011
212-253-6900
Child Actors
Full Service

INTEGRITY TALENT, INC.
165 West 46th St., Suite 1210
New York, NY 10036
212-575-5756
Full Service

INTERNATIONAL CREATIVE MANAGEMENT
40 West 57th St.
New York, NY 10019
212-556-5600
Full Service

IT MODELS/OMARS MEN
251 Fifth Ave., 7th Floor, Penthouse
New York, NY 10016
212-481-7220
Full Service

JAM THEATRICAL AGENCY, INC.
352 Seventh Ave., Suite 1500
New York, NY 10001
212-376-6330
Full Service

JAN J. AGENCY INC.
365 West 34th St., 3rd Floor
New York, NY 10001
212-967-5265
Child Actors
Full Service
Commercials
Young Adults
Theatrical

JORDAN, GILL & DORNBAUM TALENT AGENCY
156 Fifth Ave., Suite 711
New York, NY 10010
212-463-8455
212-691-6111
Child Actors
Full Service
Commercials
Theatrical

KERIN-GOLDBERG ASSOCIATES
155 East 55th St.
New York, NY 10022
212-838-7373
Full Service

ARCHER KING
10 Columbus Circle, Suite 1492
New York, NY 10019
212-765-3103
Full Service

KMA ASSOCIATES
11 Broadway Rm, Suite 1101
New York, NY 10004
212-581-4610
Full Service

THE KRASNY OFFICE INC.
1501 Broadway, Suite 1510
New York, NY 10036
212-730-8160
Full Service

LALLY TALENT AGENCY
630 Ninth Ave.
New York, NY 10036
212-974-8718
Full Service

LANTZ OFFICE
888 Seventh Ave.
New York, NY 10106
212-586-0200
Full Service

LIONEL LARNER LTD.
119 West 57th St., Suite 1412
New York, NY 10019
212-246-3105
Full Service

BRUCE LEVY AGENCY
335 West 38th St., Suite 802
New York, NY 10018
212-563-7079
Full Service

BERNARD AGENCY LIEBHABER
352 Seventh Ave.
New York, NY 10001
212-631-7561
Full Service

MCDONALD/RICHARDS MODEL MANAGEMENT, INC.
156 Fifth Ave., Suite 222
New York, NY 10010
212-627-3100
Full Service

MEREDITH MODEL MANAGEMENT
10 Furler St.
Totowa, NY 7512
212-812-0122
Full Service

WILLIAM MORRIS AGENCY, INC.
1325 Ave. Of the Americas
New York, NY 10019
212-586-5100
Full Service

NOUVELLE TALENT MANAGEMENT, INC.
20 Bethune St., Suite 3B
New York, NY 10014
212-645-0940
Full Service

OMNIPOP, INC.
55 West Old Country Road
Hicksville, NY 11801
516-937-6011
Full Service

OPPENHEIM/CHRISTIE ASSOCIATES, LTD.
13 East 37th St.
New York, NY 10016
212-213-4330
Full Service

FIFI OSCARD AGENCY, INC.
24 West 40th St., Suite 17
New York, NY 10018
212-764-1100
212-840-5019
Child Actors
Full Service
Commercials
Theatrical

HARRY PACKWOOD TALENT LTD.
250 West 57th St., Suite 2012
New York, NY 10107
212-586-8900
Full Service

DOROTHY PALMER TALENT AGENCY
235 West 56th St., Suite 24K
New York, NY 10019
212-765-4280

PARADIGM, A TALENT & LITERARY AGENCY
200 West 57th St., Suite 900
New York, NY 10019
212-246-1030
Full Service

PREMIER TALENT ASSOCIATES
3 East 54th St.
New York, NY 10022
212-758-4900
Full Service

PROFESSIONAL ARTISTS UNLTD.
513 West 54th St.
New York, NY 10019
212-247-8770
Full Service

PYRAMID ENTERTAINMENT GROUP
89 Fifth Ave.
New York, NY 10003
212-242-7274
Full Service

RACHAEL'S TALENT AGENCY, INC.
134 West 29th St., Suite 903
New York, NY 10001
212-967-0665
Full Service

RADIOACTIVE TALENT INC.
240-03 Linden Blvd.
Elmont, NY 11003
212-315-1919
Full Service

NORMAN REICH AGENCY
1650 Broadway, Suite 303
New York, NY 10019
212-399-2881
Full Service

GILLA ROOS, LTD.
16 West 22nd St., 7th Floor
New York, NY 10010
212-727-7820
Full Service

SAMES & ROLLNICK ASSOCIATES
250 West 57th St., Suite 703
New York, NY 10107
212-315-4434
Full Service

THE SANDERS AGENCY LTD.
1204 Broadway, Suite 306
New York, NY 10001
212-779-3737
Full Service

SCHIFFMAN, EKMAN, MORRISON, AND MARX
22 West 19th St., 8th Floor
New York, NY 10011
212-627-5500
Child Actors
Full Service
Commercials
Young Adults
Theatrical

WILLIAM SCHILL AGENCY INC.
250 West 57th St., Suite 2402
New York, NY 10107
212-315-5919
Full Service

SCHULLER TALENT, INC. AKA NEW YORK KIDS
276 Fifth Ave., 10th Floor
New York, NY 10001
212-532-6005
Full Service

Your Kid Ought To Be In Pictures

SHEPLIN ARTISTS & ASSOCIATES
160 Fifth Ave., Suite 909
New York, NY 10010
212-647-1311
Full Service

SILVER, MASSETTI & SZATMARY EAST ,LTD.
145 West 45th St., Suite 1204
New York, NY 10036
212-391-4545
Full Service

SPECIAL ARTISTS AGENCY, INC.
111 East 22nd St., Suite 4C
New York, NY 10010
212-420-0200
Full Service

PETER STRAIN & ASSOCIATES, INC.
1501 Broadway, Suite 2900
New York, NY 10036
212-391-0380
Full Service

TALENT REPRESENTATIVES, INC.
20 East 53rd St.
New York, NY 10022
212-752-1835
Full Service

THE TANTLEFF OFFICE
375 Greenwich St., Suite 700
New York, NY 10013
212-941-3939
Full Service

MICHAEL THOMAS AGENCY, INC.
305 Madison Ave., Suite 4419
New York, NY 10165
212-867-0303
Full Service

TRANUM, ROBERTSON, & HUGHES, INC.
2 Dag Hammarskjold Plaza
New York, NY 10017
212-371-7500
Full Service

TRAWICK ARTISTS MANAGEMENT, INC.
1926 Broadway, Suite 600
New York, NY 10023
212-874-2482
Full Service

WATERS & NICOLOSI
1501 Broadway, Suite 1305
New York, NY 10036
212-302-8787
Full Service

RUTH RUTH WEBB ENTERPRISES, INC.
445 West 45th St.
New York, NY 10036
212-757-6300
Full Service

HANNS WOLTERS THEATRICAL AGENCY
10 West 37th St.
New York, NY 10018
212-714-0100
Full Service

ANN WRIGHT REPRESENTATIVES,INC.
165 West 46th St.
New York, NY 10036
212-764-6770
Full Service

WRITERS & ARTISTS AGENCY
19 West 44th St., Suite 1000
New York, NY 10036
212-391-1112
Full Service

ZOLI MANAGEMENT, INC.
3 West 18th St., 5th Floor
New York, NY 10011
212-242-7490
Full Service

Boston Area

MODEL CLUB, INC.
229 Berkely St.
Boston, MA 2116
617-247-9020
Child Actors
Full Service

MAGGIE, INC.
35 Newbury St.
Boston, MA 2116
617-536-2639

THE MODELS GROUP
374 Congress St., Suite 305
Boston, MA 2210
617-426-4711

MODELS, INC.
218 Newbury St.
Boston, MA 2116
617-437-6212
Full Service

Chicago Area

AMBASSADOR TALENT AGENTS
333 N. Michigan Ave., Suite 314
Chicago, IL 60601
312-641-3491

ARIA MODEL & TALENT MGMT.
1017 W. Washington St., Suite 2A
Chicago, IL 60607
312-243-9400

CUNNINGHAM, ESCOTT, & DIPENE
One East Superior St., Suite 505
Chicago, IL 60611
312-944-5600
Commercials

DAVID & LEE
70 W. Hubbard St., Suite 200
Chicago, IL 60610
312-670-4444

HARRISE DAVIDSON & ASSOC.
65 E. Wacker Place, Suite 2401
Chicago, IL 60601
312-782-4480

ETA INC.
7558 S. Chicago Ave
Chicago, IL 60619
312-752-3955

THE GEDDES AGENCY
1633 N. Halsted St., Suite 400
Chicago, IL 60614
312-787-8333

SHIRLEY HAMILTON
333 E. Ontario, Suite B
Chicago, IL 60611
312-787-4700

LINDA JACK TALENT
230 East Ohio St., Suite 200
Chicago, IL 60611
312-587-1155

JEFFERSON & ASSOCIATES
1050 N. State St.
Chicago, IL 60610
312-337-1930

LILY'S TALENT AGENCY
5962 North Elston
Chicago, IL 60646
312-792-3456

EMILIA LORENCE
619 N. Wabash
Chicago, IL 60611
312-787-2033

Dallas Area

ACCLAIM PARTNERS
4107 Medical Parkway, Suite 210
Austin, TX 78756
512-323-5566
Full Service

THE CAMPBELL AGENCY
3906 Lemmon Ave., Suite 200
Dallas, TX 75219
214-522-8991

MARY C. COLLINS AGENT TALENT
5956 Sherry Lane, Suite 917
Dallas, TX 75225
214-360-0900

DANIEL-HORNE AGENCY, INC.
1576 NorthWest Hwy.
Garland, TX 75041
971-613-7827
Full Service

KIM DAWSON AGENCY
700 Tower North
2710 N. Stemmons Freeway
Dallas, TX 75207
214-630-5161

DOUBLE TAKE TALENT AGENCY
13101 Preston, Suite 300
Dallas, TX 75240
972-404-4436
Full Service

MARQUEE TALENT, INC.
5911 Maple Ave.
Dallas, TX 75235
214-357-0355
Full Service

IVETT STONE AGENCY
6309 N. O'Connor Road, Suite 100
Irving, TX 75039
972-506-9962

PEGGY TAYLOR TALENT
1825 Market Center Blvd., Suite 320A/LB37
Dallas, TX 75207
214-651-7884

San Francisco Area

BOOM MODELS & TALENT
2325 3rd St., Suite 223
San Francisco, CA 94107
415-626-6591
Full Service

COVERS MODEL & TALENT AGENCY
4716 Foulger Drive
Santa Rosa, CA 95405
707-539-9252

MARLA DELL TALENT
2124 Union St.
San Francisco, CA 94123
415-563-9213

THE E.S. TALENT AGENCY
55 New Montgomery St., Suite 511
San Francisco, CA 94105
415-543-6575

FILM THEATRE ACTORS XCHNGE
582 Market St., Suite 302
San Francisco, CA 94104
415-433-3920

THE FRAZER AGENCY
4300 Stevens Creek Blvd., Suite 126
San Jose, CA 95129
408-554-1055

LOOK MODEL & TALENT AGENCY
166 Geary Blvd., Suite 1406
San Francisco, CA 94108
415-781-2841

LOS LATINOS TALENT AGENCY/TALENT PLUS
2801 Moorpark Ave, Suite 11-Dyer Building
San Jose, CA 95128
408-296-2213

MITCHELL TALENT MANAGEMENT
323 Geary St., Suite 303
San Francisco, CA 94102
415-395-9475

PANDA AGENCY
3721 Hoen Ave.
Santa Rosa, CA 95405
707-576-0711

CLAUDIA QUINN ASSOCIATES
533 Airport Blvd., Suite 400
Burlingame, CA 94010
415-615-9950

QUINN-TONRY, INC.
601 Brannan St.
San Francisco, CA 94107
415-543-3797

SAN FRANCISCO TOP MODELS AND TALENT
870 Market St., Suite 1076
San Francisco, CA 94102
415-391-1800
Full Service

THE STARS AGENCY
777 Davis St.
San Francisco, CA 94111
415-421-6272

Arizona

ACT
6264 East Grant Road
Tucson, AZ 85712
520-885-3246
Full Service

ACTION TALENT AGENCY
2720 East Broadway
Tucson, AZ 85716
520-881-6535
Full Service

ROBERT BLACK AGENCY
7525 E. Camelback Road, Suite 200
Scottsdale, AZ 85251
602-966-2537

DANI'S AGENCY
One East Camelback Road, Suite 550
Phoenix, AZ 85012
602-263-1918

FOSI'S TALENT AGENCY
2777 N. Campbell Ave., Suite 209
Tucson, AZ 85719
520-795-3534

LEIGHTON AGENCY, INC.
2231 E. Camelback Road, Suite 319
Phoenix, AZ 85016
602-224-9255

SIGNATURE MODELS & TALENT
2600 N. 44th St., Suite 209
Phoenix, AZ 85008
602-966-1102

California

AGENCY 2 MODEL & TALENT AGENCY
2425 San Diego Ave., Suite 209
San Diego, CA 92110
619-291-9556

ARTIST MANAGEMENT, TALENT AGENCY
835 Fifth Ave., Suite 411
San Diego, CA 92101
619-233-6655
Full Service

ELEGANCE TALENT AGENCY
2763 State St.
Carlsbad, CA 92008
619-434-3397
Full Service

NOUVEAU MODEL MANAGEMENT, TALENT AGENCY
909 Prospect St., Suite 230
La Jolla, CA 91037
619-456-1400
Full Service

SAN DIEGO MODEL MANAGEMENT
824 Camino Del Rio North, Suite 552
San Diego, CA 92108
619-296-1018
Full Service

SHAMON FREITAS & COMPANY
9606 Tierra Grande St., Suite 204
San Diego, CA 92126
619-549-3955
Full Service

Colorado

DONNA BALDWIN TALENT
50 South Steele St., Suite 260
Denver, CO 80209
303-320-0067

BARBIZON AGENCY
7535 E. Hampden, Suite 108
Denver, CO 80231
303-337-6952

MATTAS THEATRICAL AGENCY
1026 W. Colorado Ave.
Colorado Springs, CO 80904
303-577-4704

MAXIMUM TALENT, INC.
3900 East Mexico Ave., Suite 105
Denver, CO 80210
303-691-2344
Full Service

VOICE CHOICE
1805 S. Bellaire St., Suite 130
Denver, CO 80222
303-756-9055
Full Service

Florida

A-1 PEG'S TALENT AGENCY
133 E. Lauren Court
FernPark, FL 32730
407-834-0406

ACT ONE TALENT AGENCY
1205 Washington Ave.
Miami Beach, FL 33139
305-672-0200

ALEXA MODEL & TALENT
4100 W. Kennedy Blvd., Suite 228
Tampa, FL 33609
813-289-8020

236

AZUREE MODELING AND TALENT
140 N. Orlando Ave, Suite 120
Winter Park, FL 32789
407-629-5025

SANDI BELL TALENT AGENCY
2582 S. Maguire Road, Suite 171
Ocoee, FL 34761
407-656-0053

BERG TALENT & MODEL AGENCY
3825 Henderson Blvd., Suite 305 A
Tampa, FL 33629
813-877-5533

BOCA TALENT & MODEL AGENCY
851 N. Market St.
Jacksonville, FL 32202
904-356-4244

BOCA TALENT AND MODEL AGENCY
829 SE 9th St.
Deerfield Beach, FL 33441
954-428-4677
Full Service

BREVARD TALENT GROUP, INC.
405 Palm Springs Blvd.
Indian Harbour Beach, FL 32937
407-773-1355

DOTT BURNS MODEL & TALENT
478 Severn Ave.
Davis Island
Tampa, FL 33606
813-251-5882

THE CHRISTENSEN GROUP
120 International Parkway, Suite 262
Heathrow, FL 32746
407-333-2506

COCONUT GROVE TALENT AGENCY
3525 Vista Court
Coconut Grove, FL 33133
305-858-3002

DIMENSIONS 3 MODELING
5205 S. Orange Ave., Suite 209
Orlando, FL 32809
407-851-2575

FAMOUS FACES ENT CO
2013 Harding St
Hollywood, FL 33020
954-922-0700

FLICK EAST -WEST TALENTS, INC.
919 Collins Ave
Miami Beach, FL 33139
305-674-9900

FLORIDA STARS MODEL & TALENT
225 West University Ave., Suite A
Gainesville, FL 32601
352-338-1086
Full Service

GREEN AGENCY, INC.
1688 Meridian Ave., 8th Floor
Miami Beach, FL 33139
305-532-9774

SUZANNE HALEY TALENT
618 Wymore Rd., Suite 2
Winter Park, FL 32789
407-644-0600

HURT-GARVER TALENT
400 N. New York Ave., Suite 207
Winter Park, FL 32789
407-740-5700

INTERNATIONAL ARTISTS GROUP, INC.
420 Lincoln Road, Suite 382
Miami Beach, FL 33139
305-538-6100

LOUISE'S PEOPLE MODEL & TALENT AGENCY
863 13th Ave. North
St. Petersburg, FL 33701
813-823-7828
Full Service

IRENE MARIE AGENCY
728 Ocean Drive
MiamiBeach, FL 33139
305-672-2929

MARTIN & DONALD TALENT AGENCY, INC.
1915-A Hollywood Blvd.
Hollywood, FL 33020
954-921-2427
Full Service

ROXANNE MCMILLAN TALENT AGENCY
12100 NE 16th Ave., Suite 106
North Miami, FL 33161

305-PAGE PARKES MODELS
660 Ocean Drive
MiamiBeach, FL 33139
305-672-4869

MARIAN POLAN TALENT AGENCY
10 Ne 11th Ave.
Ft. Lauderdale, FL 33301
954-525-8351

MICHELE POMMIER MODELS INC.
81 Washington Ave.
MiamiBeach, FL 33139
305-672-9344

SHEFFIELD AGENCY, INC.
800 West Ave., Suite C-1
MiamiBeach, FL 33139
305-531-5886
Full Service

STELLAR TALENT AGENCY
407 Lincoln Road, Suite 2K
MiamiBeach, FL 33139
305-672-2217

EVELYN STEWART'S MODELING
1765-B West Fletcher Ave.
Tampa, FL 33612
813-968-1441

WORLD OF KIDS INC.
1460 Ocean Drive, Suite 205
MiamiBeach, FL 33139
305-672-5437

Georgia

ATLANTA MODELS & TALENT, INC.
2970 Peachtree Road NW, Suite 660
Atlanta, GA 30305
404-261-9627
Full Service

AW/ATLANTA
887 West Marietta St., Suite N-101
Atlanta, GA 30318
404-876-8555
Full Service

TED BORDEN & ASSOC.IATES
2434 Adina Drive NE, Suite B
Atlanta, GA 30324
404-266-0664

THE BURNS AGENCY
602 Hammett Drive
Decatur, GA 30032
404-299-8114
Full Service

ELITE MODEL MANAGEMENT CORP/ATLANTA
181 14th St., Suite 325
Atlanta, GA 30309
404-872-7444
Full Service

GENESIS MODELS AND TALENT, INC.
1465 Northside Drive, Suite 120
Atlanta, GA 30318
404-350-9212
Full Service

GLYN KENNEDY MODELS & TALENT
3500 Emperor Way
Atlanta, GA 30084
770-908-9082
Full Service

THE PEOPLE STORE
2004 Rockledge Road NE, Suite 60
Atlanta, GA 30324
404-874-6448

DONNA SUMMERS' TALENT
8950 Laurel Way, Suite 200
Alpharetta, GA 30202
770-518-9855

Hawaii

ADR MODEL & TALENT AGENCY
431 Kuwili St.
Honolulu, HI 96817
808-524-4777
Full Service

AMOS KOTOMORI AGENT SERVICES
1018 Hoawa Lane
Honolulu, HI 96826
808-955-6511
Full Service

KATHY MULLER TALENT AGENCY
619 Kapahulu Ave., Penthouse
Honolulu, HI 96815
808-737-7917
Full Service

Illinois

NORTH SHORE TALENT, INC.
450 Peterson Road
Libertyville, IL 60048
847-816-1811

SA-RAH
1935 S. Halsted, Suite 301
Chicago, IL 60608
312-733-2822

SALAZAR & NAVAS, INC.
760 N. Ogden Ave, Suite 2200
Chicago, IL 60622
312-751-3419

NORMAN SCHUCART ENTERPRISES
1417 Green Bay Rd
Highland Park, IL 60035
847-433-1113

STEWART TALENT MANAGEMENT
212 W. Superior St.,Suite 406
Chicago, IL 60610
312-943-3131

SUSANNE'S A-PLUS TALENT
108 W. Oak St.
Chicago, IL 60610
312-943-8315

VOICES UNLIMITED, INC.
541 N. Fairbanks Ct., Suite 28
Chicago, IL 60611
312-642-3262

ARLENE WILSON TALENT
430 W. Erie St., Suite 210
Chicago, IL 60610
312-573-0200

Indiana

CJ MERCURY, INC.
1330 Lake Ave.
Whiting, IN 46394
219-659-2701

Kansas

JACKSON ARTISTS
7251 Lowell Dr, Suite 200
Overland Park, KS 66204
913-384-6688

TALENT UNLIMITED, LLC
4049 Pennsylvania, Suite 300
Kansas City, KS 64111
816-561-9040
Full Service

Maryland

FOX ENTERPRISES, INC.
7700 Little River Pike, Suite 200
Annandale, MD 22003
703-506-0335
Full Service

KIDS INTERNATIONAL TALENT AGENCY
938 East Swan Creek Rd., Suite 152
Ft. Washington, MD 20744
301-292-6093
Full Service

TAYLOR ROYALL AGENCY
2308 South Road
Baltimore, MD 21209
410-466-5959

Michigan

AFFILIATED MODELS INC.
1680 Crooks Road, Suite 200
Troy, MI 48084
810-244-8770

PRODUCTIONS PLUS
30600 Telegraph Road, Suite 2156
Birmingham, MI 48025
810-644-5566

THE TALENT SHOP
30100 Telegraph Road, Suite 116
Birmingham, MI 48025
810-644-4877
Full Service

THE I GROUP, LLC
28880 Southfield Road, Suite 281
Lathrup Village, MI 48076
810-552-8842
Full Service

Missouri

TALENT PLUS, INC.
55 Maryland Plaza
St. Louis, MO 63108
314-367-5588

Nevada

J BASKOW & ASSOC.IATES
2948 E. Russell Rd.
Las Vegas, NV 89120
702-733-7818
Full Service

CREATIVE TALENT AGENCY
900 E. Karen Ave., Suite D-116
Las Vegas, NV 89109
702-737-0611
Full Service

LENZ AGENCY
1591 East Desert Inn Road
Las Vegas, NV 89109
702-733-6888
Full Service

DONNA WAUHOB AGENCY
3135 Industrial Road, Suite 234
Las Vegas, NV 89109
702-733-1017
Full Service

New Jersey

VERONICA GOODMAN AGENCY
411 Route 70 East ,Suite 240
Cherry Hills, NJ 8034
609-795-3133
Full Service

McCULLOUGH ASSOC.IATES
8 South Hanover Ave.
Margate, NJ 8402
609-822-2222
Full Service

New Mexico

AESTHETICS, INC.
489 1/2 Don Miguel
Santa Fe, NM 87501
505-982-5883
Full Service

APPLAUSE TALENT AGENCY
225 San Pedro NE
Albuquerque, NM 87108
505-262-9733

CIMARRON TALENT AGENCY
10605 Casador Del Oso NE
Albuquerque, NM 87111
505-292-2314

EATON AGENCY, INC.
3636 High St. N. E
Albuquerque, NM 87107
505-344-3149

FLAIR MODELING & TALENT
3901 Indian School Road NE, Suite D-107
Albuquerque, NM 87110
505-881-4688
Full Service

THE MANNEQUIN AGENCY
2021 San Mateo Blvd. Ne
Albuquerque, NM 87110
505-266-6823

THE PHOENIX AGENCY
6400 Uptown Blvd. NE, Suite 481-W
Albuquerque, NM 87110
505-881-1209

SOUTH OF SANTA FE TALENT GUILD, INC.
6921-B Montgomery NE
Albuquerque, NM 87109
505-880-8550
Full Service

Oregon

CUSICK'S TALENT MANAGEMENT
1009 N.W. Hoyt St., Suite 100
Portland, OR 97209
503-274-8555
Full Service

Pennsylvania

DENNISE ASKINS
New Market, Suite 200-Head House Square
Philadelphia, PA 19147
215-925-7795

THE CLARO MODELING AGENCY
1513 West Passyunk Ave
Philadelphia, PA 19145
215-465-7788

EXPRESSIONS MODELING & TALENT
110 Church St.
Philadelphia, PA 19106
215-923-4420

LANGE GREER & ASSOC.IATES
18 Great Valley Parkway, Suite 180
Malvern, PA 19355
215-647-5515

PLAZA 7
160 N. Gulph Road
King Of Prussia, PA 19406
610-337-2693

REINHARD. AGENCY
2021 Arch St., Suite 400
Philadelphia, PA 19103
215-567-2008

THE T.G. AGENCY
2820 Smallman St.
Pittsburgh, PA 15222
412-471-8011
Full Service

Tennessee

ACTOR AND OTHERS TALENT AGENCY
6676 Memphis-Arlington Road
Bartlett, TN 38134
901-385-7885
Full Service

BOX OFFICE, INC. TALENT AGENCY
1010 16th Ave. South
Nashville, TN 37212
615-256-5400
Full Service

CREATIVE ARTISTS AGENCY, INC.
3310 West End Ave., 5th Floor
Nashville, TN 37203
615-383-8787
Full Service

BUDDY LEE ATTRACTIONS
38 Music Square East ,Suite 300
Nashville, TN 37203
615-244-4336

WILLIAM MORRIS AGENCY
2100 W. End Ave., Suite 1000
Nashville, TN 37203
615-385-0310
Full Service

TALENT & MODEL LAND
4516 Granny White Pike
Nashville, TN 37204
615-321-5596

TALENT TREK AGENC
406 11th St.
Knoxville, TN 37916
423-977-8735

Texas

ACCLAIM PARTNERS
4107 Medical Parkway, Suite 207
Austin, TX 78756
512-323-5566
Full Service

ACTORS, ETC
2620 Fountainview, Suite 210
Houston, TX 77057
713-785-4495

INTERMEDIA TALENT AGENCY
5353 W. Alabama, Suite 222
Houston, TX 77056
713-622-8282

PASTORINI BOSBY TALENT AG
3013 Fountain View Drive, Suite 240
Houston, TX 77057
713-266-4488

QUAID TALENT AGENCY
5959 Richmond, Suite 310
Houston, TX 77057
713-975-9600
Full Service

SHERRY YOUNG AGENCY
2620 Fountain View, Suite 212
Houston, TX 77057
713-266-5800

Washington

ACTORS GROUP
114 Alaskan Way South, Suite 104
Seattle, WA 98104
206-624-9465

E THOMAS BLISS & ASSOC.IATES, INC.
219 1St.Ave. South, Suite 420
Seattle, WA 98104
206-340-1875
Full Service

DRAMATIC ARTISTS AGENCY
1000 Lenora St., Suite 501
Seattle, WA 98121
206-442-9190
Full Service

LOLA HALLOWELL AGENCY
1700 West lake Ave North, Suite 600
Seattle, WA 98109
206-281-4646

CAROL JAMES AGENCY
117 S. Main St
Seattle, WA 98104
206-447-9191

Washington, DC

CENTRAL AGENCY
623 Pennsylvania Ave. SE
Washington, DC 20003
202-547-6300

State Labor Offices

ALABAMA Department of Industrial Relations
649 Monroe St.
Montgomery, AL 36131
334-353-3580

ALASKA Labor Standards and Safety Division
Department of Labor
3301 Eagle St., #301
Anchorage, AK 99510
907-465-4855

ARIZONA State Labor Department
800 W. Washington St. #102
Phoenix, AZ 85005
602-542-4515

ARKANSAS Department of Labor
Labor Standards Division
1022 High Street
Little Rock, AR 72202
501-682-4500

CALIFORNIA Division of Labor Standards Enforcement
6150 Van Nuys Blvd., #100
Van Nuys, CA 91401
818-901-5312

CANADA ACTRA
1414 - 8111 St. S.W.
Calgary, Alberta T2R 1J6
403-228-3123

COLORADO Department of Labor and Industry
Labor Standards Unit
1120 Lincoln Ave., #1302
Denver, CO 80203-2140
303-572-2241

CONNECTICUT Department of Labor
200 Folly Brook Building
Wethersfield, CT 06109
860-566-5160

DELAWARE
302-761-8020

DISTRICT OF COLUMBIA Washington, D.C. Film Office
717- 14th Street N.W., 10th Floor
Washington, D.C. 20005
202-727-6608

FLORIDA Division of Labor
Child Labor Section
2002 Old St. Augustine Rd.
Bldg. E, Suite 45
Tallahassee, FL 32399-0663
904-488-3044

GEORGIA Department of Labor
Child Labor Unit
148 International Blvd.
Atlanta, GA 30303-1751
404-656-3177

HAWAII Department of Labor and Industrial Relations
Division of Labor
Honolulu, HI 96813
808-586-8778

IDAHO Department of Labor
317 Main St.
Boise, ID 83735-0600
208-334-67252

ILLINOIS Department of Labor
Work Permit Office
1819 W. Pershing Road
Chicago, IL 60609
312-793-2800

INDIANA The Bureau of Child Labor
Department of Labor
1013 State Office Building
Indianapolis, IN 46204
317-232-2675

IOWA Division of Labor
Child Labor Division
1000 E. Grand Ave.
Des Moines, IA 50319
515-281-3606

KANSAS Kansas Film Commission
700 S.W. Harrison St. #1200
Topeka, KS 66603-3712
913-296-4927

KENTUCKY Kentucky Film Commission
Capitol Plaza Tower, 22nd Floor
500 Mero Street
Frankfort, KY 40601
502-564-3456

LOUISIANA Dept. of Labor
P.O. Box 94094
Baton Rouge, LA 70804
504-342-3111

MAINE Bureau of Labor Standards
Division of Minimum Wage and Child Labor
Augusta, ME 04330
207-624-6410

MARYLAND Department of Licensing and Regulation
Division of Labor and Industry
501 St. Paul Place
Baltimore, MD 21203
301-333-4196

MASSACHUSETTS Division of Occupational Safety
State Capitol
Boston, MA 02202
617-727-3452

MICHIGAN Department of Labor
Bureau of Employment Standards
7150 Harris Drive
Lansing, MI 48909
517-322-1825

MINNESOTA Department of Labor and Industry
443 Lafayette Road
St. Paul, MN 55101
612-296-2282

245

Your Kid Ought To Be In Pictures

MISSISSIPPI Mississippi Film Office
1200 Walter Sillers Bldg.
Jackson, MS 39205
601-359-3297

MISSOURI Department of Labor and Industrial Relations
Division of Labor Standards
3315 W. Truman Blvd.
Jefferson City, MO 65102-0449
573-751-3403

MONTANA Department of Labor and Industry
1805 Prospect Street
Helena, MT 59624
406-444-5600

NEBRASKA Department of Labor Safety Division
State Office Bldg., 3rd Floor
1313 Farnum St.
Omaha, NE 68102
402-595-3095

NEVADA Department of Labor
Capitol Complex
Carson City, NV 89710
702-687-4850

NEW HAMPSHIRE Department of Labor
Manchester, NH 03101
603-271-3176

NEW JERSEY Department of Labor
Division of Workplace Standards
Office of Wages and Hour Compliance
Trenton, NJ 08625
609-292-2337

NEW MEXICO State Labor and Industrial Commission
1596 Pacheco St.
Santa Fe, NM 87501
505-827-6875

NEW YORK
Human Resources Administration
Department of Social Services
Special Services for Children
80 Lafayette St., New York, NY 10013
718-291-1900

NORTH CAROLINA Department of Labor
Labor Building
4 West Edenton Street
Raleigh, NC 27611
919-733-2152

NORTH DAKOTA Department of Labor
600 E. Boulevard, 6th Floor
Bismarck, ND 58505
701-328-2660

OHIO Department of Industrial Relations
Columbus, OH 43215
614-644-2239

OKLAHOMA Department of Labor
4001 North Lincoln Blvd.
Oklahoma City, OK 73105-5212
405-528-1500

OREGON Bureau of Labor and Industries
Wage and Hour Division
800 N.E. Oregon Street, #32
Portland, OR 97232
503-731-4074

PENNSYLVANIA Bureau of Labor Standards
1305 Labor and Industry Bldg.
Harrisburg, PA 17120
717-787-4670

RHODE ISLAND Department of Labor
Codes Section
220 Elmwood Ave.
Providence, RI 02907
401-457-1800

SOUTH CAROLINA Department of Labor
3600 Forest Drive
Columbia, SC 29211-1329
803-896-4300

SOUTH DAKOTA Department of Labor
Pierre, SD 57501
605-773-3681

TENNESSEE Department of Labor
501 Union Building
Nashville, TN 37219
615-741-2582

TEXAS Department of Labor Standards
Austin, TX 78767
512-794-1180

U.S. VIRGIN ISLANDS Department of Labor
Charlotte Amalie
St. Thomas, USVI 00610
809-776-3700

UTAH Utah Industrial Commission
160 E. 300 South
Salt Lake City, UT 84110
801-530-6801

VERMONT Department of Labor and Industry
Wage and Hour Division
120 State Street
Montpelier, VT 05602
802-828-2157

VIRGINIA Department of Labor and Industry
Division of State Labor Law Administration
13 South 13th Street
Richmond, VA 23219
804-786-2386

WASHINGTON Department of Labor and Industries
Supervisor of Employment Standards
General Administration Building
Olympia, WA 98504
360-902-5316

WEST VIRGINIA Department of Labor
1800 Washington St. East
Charleston, WV 25304
304-558-7890

WISCONSIN Department of Labor
Madison, WI 53707
608-266-6860

WYOMING Labor Commission
Cheyenne, WY 82002
307-777-7262

Glossary

action. The word used by the director to start the cameras rolling and the actors acting.

AFTRA. American Federation of Television and Radio Artists. One of two—the other is SAG—unions (guilds) for actors in television and radio.

agent/agency. A person or company hired by an actor to obtain work in the industry.

audition. A meeting or interview between a casting company or person and the actor.

back-up kids. SAG child actors hired to fill in for very young actors in case the young actors cannot fulfill their job obligations.

book. The word used to describe an actor being hired for a job.

breakdowns. Sheets sent daily to agents, comprised of character descriptions in search of actors to play them.

call. An audition.

callback. A second audition.

casting director. The person casting a project.

composite. A photographic 8 x 10 consisting of several pictures of the same actor.

Coogan Law, The. The law established by California to ensure that child actors and their money are protected.

crew. The people hired to do work on a production.

cut. The word used by the director to stop the cameras from rolling and the actors from acting.

dailies. The work shot on any given day, which is reviewed by the producers and director.

dialogue. The words spoken by the actors.

direction. The movement the actors are given by the director.

director. The person of a production, who gives the actors direction and motivation.

emancipated adult. A child under the age of eighteen who is declared an adult by the courts.

extra. A person hired to play an incidental, background character in a production; the extra has no scripted lines.

first call. The first time an actor auditions for a project.

first look. The casting director's term for the first time an actor auditions.

franchised agency. An agency registered with the Screen Actors Guild.

gimmick. Anything that sets one actor apart from another; usually, it's something physical (sometimes called "business").

Guild, The. The Screen Actors Guild.

head shot. A photograph of the actor's head and/or upper torso.

improvisation. Unscripted dialogue and direction the actor creates on the spur of the moment.

lines. Dialogue that is scripted for the actor to say.

location. Principal photography that takes place out of town.

looping. Putting an actor's voice on a track to match a piece of existing film.

manager. Someone who handles the business affairs of an actor.

mark. The exact place where the actor should stand before the director yells "Action."

media. The press.

minor. A child under the age of eighteen.

M.O.W. A two-hour movie of the week, made for television.

pay autho. An authorization form signed by the actor to allow his agent to deposit his check into the agency's account.

pilot. The first episode of a series.

places, please. The words used by the director to the actors to go where he wants them to stand; said before he yells, "Action."

press. See media.

principal performer. The main characters (actors) of a production.

principal photography. The actual filming of a production.

print. The words used by the director if he is satisfied with the scene captured on film.

producer. The person who finances a production.

publicist. The person who handles publicity for a production or an actor.

representation. The relationship between actor and agent.

rolling. What the camera is doing while filming the scene.

SAG. The Screen Actors Guild.

set. The place where the actors act during filming.

settle, people. The words used by the director when he wants the set to be quiet.

shoot. Principal photography.

sides. The dialogue any single actor says in a production.

sign-in/sign-out sheet. Where the actor writes his name to let the casting people know he has arrived at an audition and the time he leaves the audition.

size sheet. The actor fills this out so the wardrobe people know his sizes.

slate. An actor's sign-in procedure before he is filmed at an audition.

social security card. The government's required number before wages are paid.

social worker. See Studio Teacher.

storyboard. The outline of a script, told in hand-drawn pictures, indicating the characters and action.

studio teacher. The person hired by the state to teach your child and to monitor state-required regulations.

submissions. Pictures and resumes of actors sent to casting companies by agents.

Taft-Hartley. A bill allowing any actor to work his first SAG job without joining the union.

trades. Papers and magazines relating specifically to the industry (i.e., *The Hollywood Reporter* and *Variety*.)

voice-over. Vocal track used on animated projects, radio or television commercials.

wardrobe. Costumes the actors wear during filming.

work permit. The document required for minors by the state.

wrap. The word used by the director when filming comes to an end (usually, "That's a wrap").

Index

About The Authors

KELLY FORD KIDWELL hails from a show business family . . . A LARGE show business family. Kelly's father was a professional comedy writer and her mother was a radio singer. Along with her six siblings, Kelly enjoyed a career in the industry as an actress and singer for most of her life. When she met and married her husband, Ron Kidwell, she traded in the spotlight and her career as a performer to settle down with Ron and raise a family. At least that's what she started out to do. Kelly is now a screenwriter and the mother of three show business children, a son and identical twin daughters, who are currently enjoying careers of their own in the industry. Above and beyond managing her own career, Kelly and Ron now juggle their schedules with the daily demands of their children's careers.

John, Hillary and Melissa's professional lives add to the family's schedule a never-ending list of interviews, callbacks, project meetings, wardrobe fittings, lessons, rehearsals, photo sessions, travel and—of course—professional shoots! Impossible, you say? That's too much stuff? It can't be done? Sure, it can. All you need is a little help. And Kelly has help—from her husband, her mother, her sisters, her brothers, their families, her friends and their families and friends and every now and then, a few people she hardly knows. Kelly will be the first to admit that without them, she would not make it through a single day . . . let alone have found the time to write this book!

RUTH DEVORIN began her career as a dancer, acrobat and tumbler, dancing in Lowe's Circuit Theaters. She continued her study of dance and voice into her teen years, eventually studying opera and musical comedy which ultimately led to her career as a standby artist for Rodgers and Hammerstein. As a young adult, she made the big move from New York to Hollywood where she was screen-tested by a major Hollywood studio, met her husband-to-be, and began yet another career as wife and, eventually, the mother of five children (all of whom enjoyed successful careers in the industry). The rest was inevitable. Two careers were combined into one, and Ruth became—and remains today—a loving mother and a devoted and caring talent agent for young performers.

Ruth has discovered and worked with: David Harper (Jim Bob on *The Waltons*), Heather O'Rourke (*Happy Days*; *Poltergeist*), Shannon Doherty (*Beverly Hills 90201*), Stanley Livingston (*My Three Sons*), Stephen Dorff (*The Gate*, his first major film role), Melora Hardin, Heather Rattray, Michelle Livingston and Sean Manning (*Toma*), Burt Ward (*Batman*). Upcoming stars on Ruth's client roster are: Robert Gavin (*Land of the Lost*), Raushan Hammond (*Hook*), and Luke Rossi (*thirtysomething*). Kelly Kidwell and Ruth Devorin met more than twenty-five years ago when Ruth represented Kelly as a young performer. Today, Ruth continues to represent many young actors who are enjoying successful careers in the industry, among them, Kelly's children, John, Hillary and Melissa.